Amazons!

The men advanced upon their female adversaries, clenched fists ready to deliver incapacitating blows. Shirl and Darleen stood their ground. Kronos launched what should have been a devastating swipe, that would have been one had it connected. But Shirl little more than shrugged and the fist missed her left ear by considerably more than the thickness of a coat of paint. And then she was on him, her own fists pummeling his chest and belly. He roared with rage and tried to throw his thick arms about her. She danced back and he embraced nothingness. What happened next was almost too fast for the eye to follow. She jumped straight up and drove both feet into his midsection. She and Kronos hit the sand simultaneously, she in a crouching posture, he flat on his back. He stirred feebly, made an attempt to get up and then slumped.

Meanwhile Darleen was disposing of her own adversary by more orthodox means, using fists only. It was a classical knock-out.

THE LAST AMAZON

A. Bertram Chandler

DAW Books, Inc.
Donald A. Wollheim, Publisher
1633 Broadway, New York, N.Y. 10019

PUBLISHED BY
THE NEW AMERICAN LIBRARY
OF CANADA LIMITED

For Susan, who makes me keep my nose
to the grindstone.

First Printing, June 1984

2 3 4 5 6 7 8 9

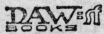 DAW TRADEMARK REGISTERED
U.S. PAT. OFF. MARCA REGISTRADA.
HECHO EN WINNIPEG, CANADA

PRINTED IN CANADA
COVER PRINTED IN U.S.A.

Chapter 1

The bands played and the Federation Survey Service Marines paraded in their scarlet and gold dress uniforms and the children waved their little flags and the grown-ups lifted high their broad-brimmed black hats as Grimes, ex-Governor John Grimes, arrived at Port Libertad, there to embark aboard the star tramp *Rim Wayfarer*. With him, to see him off, were two people whom he did not regard as friends—but protocol demanded their attendance. One of them was Estrelita O'Higgins, still, despite all, President of Liberia. She was a survivor, that one. She had contrived to lay the blame for all of the planet's troubles, culminating in the armed revolt against the Earth-appointed Governor, Grimes, on the now disgraced Colonel Bardon, lately commanding officer of the Terran garrison. The other was Captain Francis Delamere, of the Federation Survey Service, the new Governor.

Delamere should have a far easier time of it than either Grimes or his immediate predecessor. He had brought his own garrison troops out with him, a large detachment of Marines who—in theory at least—gave their allegiance to the senior Terran naval officer on Liberia, Captain Delamere. And almost immediately after his arrival (he was a notorious ladies' man) he had made a big hit with the President. For him the job should be a sinecure. Even he would find it hard to make a mess of it—as long as he did not try to interfere with the smooth running of the machinery of government that Grimes—who was for a while, after the putting down of the rebellion, de facto dictator—had set up, with able, honest and dedicated men and women in all the key positions.

But Frankie, thought Grimes, would find it hard to keep his meddling paws off things. He had tried to take an officious interest in Grimes' own affairs even before the formal handing-over ceremonies, had made it plain that he wanted his old enemy off the premises as soon as possible, if not before, so that he could bask in his new gubernatorial glory.

He had said, in his most supercilious manner, "There's no need for you to hang around here like a bad smell, Grimes."

"But I thought that you were keeping *Orion* here for a while," said Grimes. "Wise of you, Frankie. During my spell as Governor I could have done with a Constellation Class cruiser sitting in my back yard."

"Who said anything about *Orion*, Grimes? I came here with a squadron."

"A *squadron?*" echoed Grimes. "Two ships. One cruiser and one Serpent Class courier . . ."

"I was forgetting," sneered Delamere, "that you're something of an expert on squadrons. Didn't you command one when you were a pirate commodore?"

"A privateer," growled Grimes. "Not a pirate."

"And now an ex-Governor," Delamere reminded him. "As such, you're entitled to a free trip back to Earth . . ."

"Not in a flying sardine can."

"Beggars can't be choosers, Grimes. Anyhow, the sooner you're back the sooner you'll be able to find another job. If anybody wants you, that is. You can't hope to get another command, not even of that *Saucy Sue* of yours."

"*Sister Sue,*" Grimes corrected him stiffly.

"What's in a name? As far as I know your Certificate of Competency has not been restored—and you'd need that, wouldn't you, even as a bold buccaneer."

"I've already told you once that I was a privateer."

"Even so, you were bloody lucky not to be hanged from your own yardarm for piracy. That judge, at the Court of Inquiry, was far too lenient. Did you slip him a backhander out of your ill-gotten gains?"

Grimes ignored this. "Anyhow," he said smugly, "I now, once again, hold a valid Certificate of Competency as Master of an Interstellar Vessel."

"What! Don't tell me that it *has* been restored to you!"

"No. It's a new one. Liberian."

"And you say it's valid? Oh, I suppose that *you* signed it, as Governor, after examining yourself."

"If you must know, it is signed by the Liberian Minister of Space Shipping. And I was examined, and passed, by the Examiner of Masters and Mates. I admit that she was appointed by myself, for that purpose. But it's a valid Certificate, recognized as such throughout the Galaxy."

"You're a cunning bastard," whispered Delamere, not without envy.

"I am when I have to be," Grimes told him. "And now all that I have to do is to catch up with *Sister Sue* and get my name back on the Register."

"I'm not letting you have that courier to take on a wild goose chase," snarled Delamere.

"I've already told you that I have no intention of traveling in the bloody thing. I'm quite capable of making my own arrangements. I know where I want to go and I know which ship, due here in a couple of days' time, will be heading in the right direction when she's finished discharging and loading."

And so the bands were playing and the Marines, in their full dress scarlet and gold, were drawn up to stiff attention with gleaming arms presented and the children were waving their little flags and the grown-ups were raising their broad-brimmed black hats high in the air as the big ground car rolled slowly up to the foot of *Rim Wayfarer*'s ramp.

Delamere's aide, a young Survey Service Lieutenant, got down from the front seat where he had been sitting beside the Marine corporal driver. He flung open a rear door with a flourish. Estrelita O'Higgins was the first out, tall in superbly tailored, well-filled denim with a scarlet neckerchief at her throat. She was as darkly handsome as when Grimes had first met her, on his arrival at this spaceport (how long ago?) but then he had been prepared to like her, to work with her. Now he knew too much about her—and she about him. Some applause greeted her appearance but it was restrained.

Delamere was next out. He wore full ceremonial rig—the gray trousers, the black morning coat, the gray silk top hat—far more happily than Grimes ever had done. In uniform Handsome Frankie, as he was derisively known, looked as though he were posing for a Survey Service recruiting poster. Now he looked as though he were posing for a Diplomatic Service recruiting poster. He took his stance alongside the President. The impression they conveyed was that of husband and wife about to see off a house guest who had outstayed his welcome.

Again there was a spatter of applause.

Grimes disembarked.

This day he was dressed for comfort—and also in accordance with local sartorial tradition. He was wearing faded blue denim, a scarlet neckerchief, a broad-brimmed black hat.

The cheers, the shouts of "Viva Grimes! Viva Grimes!" were deafening. The Marine band struck up the retiring Governor's own national song, "Waltzing Matilda." Both Delamere and the President frowned. This was not supposed to be an item on the agenda—but Colonel Grant, commanding officer of the Marines, had known Grimes before his resignation from the Survey Service.

The people were singing that good old song.

And soon, thought Grimes, *there'll be only my ghost to haunt this billabong. . . .*

Estrelita O'Higgins extended her long-fingered right hand, palm down. Grimes bowed to kiss it. She whispered something. It sounded like, "Don't come back, you bastard!" Francis Delamere raised his silk hat. Grimes raised his felt hat. Neither man attempted to shake hands.

Slowly Grimes walked up the ramp to the after airlock of *Rim Wayfarer*. At the head of the gangway the master, Captain Gunning, smart enough in his dress black and gold, was waiting to receive him.

He saluted with what was probably deliberate sloppiness and said, "Glad to have you aboard, Commodore."

"I'm glad to be aboard, Captain," said Grimes.

"I bet you are. It must be a relief to get away from the stuffed shirts."

"The era of the stuffed shirt is just beginning here," Grimes told him.

Gunning, looking down at the new Governor standing stiffly beside the President, laughed. "I see what you mean."

Grimes turned, to wave for the last time to those who had been his people. They waved back, all of them, native Liberians and those who, as refugees from all manner of disasters, had sought and found a new home on Liberia.

"Viva Grimes! Viva Grimes!"

"I hate to interrupt, Commodore," said Gunning, "but it's time that I was getting the old girl upstairs."

"She's your ship, Captain."

"But what a send-off! Those people sound as though they're really sorry to lose you."

"Quite a few," Grimes told him with a grin, "will be glad to see the back of me."

"I can imagine."

The two men stepped into the elevator cage that would carry them up to the control room. The ramp retracted and the outer and inner airlock doors closed.

In less than five minutes *Rim Wayfarer* was lifting into the clear, noonday sky.

Chapter 2

Grimes and Gunning were at ease in the master's day cabin, enjoying a few drinks and a yarn before dinner. Trajectory had been set, all life support systems were functioning perfectly, the light lunch served as soon as possible after lift-off had been a good one and Grimes was looking forward to the evening meal.

It was good to be back aboard a ship again, he was thinking as he sipped his pink gin, even though it was only as a passenger. Still, he was a privileged one, being treated more as a guest.

"You know Sparta, of course," said Gunning.

"I was only there the once," said Grimes. "Years ago. When I was captain of the Federation Survey Service census ship *Seeker*."

Gunning laughed. "But you must know *something* about Sparta. Every time that I'm sent to a planet I haven't been to before I do some swotting up on it. There's not much information in the ship's library data bank—just the coordinates and a few details about climate and such. Rim Runners don't believe in paying good money for what they, in their wisdom, regard as useless information. But I found the Libertad Public Library quite informative. Historical details—from the time of *Doric*'s landing to the present. The way Sparta was dragged into the political framework of the Federation—and the way a certain Lieutenant Commander John Grimes initiated this process."

"I was just there when it happened," said Grimes. "Or when it started to happen. I was little more than a spectator."

"As you were on Liberia, Commodore, when things happened." Gunning laughed. "I'd just hate to be around when you were something more than just a spectator."

"But I was little more on Sparta," Grimes insisted. "One of my scientific officers, Maggie Lazenby, was the prime mover. She took a shine to Brasidus, who is now the Archon, and he to her." He laughed. "It was the first time that he'd had any

9

dealings with a woman. He really thought that she was a member of some alien species. . . .''

"I've often thought the same myself about women," said Gunning. "But that must have been a weird state of affairs on Sparta when you landed there."

"It was," reminisced Grimes. "It was. An all-male population, with all that that implies. Babies—male babies only—produced by the so-called Birth Machine. A completely spurious but quite convincing biology taught in the schools to make sense of this. The planet was a Lost Colony, of course, founded during the First Expansion. You know, the Deep Freeze ships. They started off with an incubator and a supply of fertilized ova. Male ova. The first King, who had been master of the starship, made sure of that. He didn't like women. He tried to model his realm on ancient Sparta but with one great improvement. Men Only. I suppose that when the original supply of ova ran out the Spartans might have had to resort to cloning but, before this came to pass, the people of another Lost Colony, Latterhaven, made contact. Trade developed between the two worlds. Fertilized human ova in exchange for spices and such."

"I got most of that from the library at Port Libertad," said Gunning. "But what was it like? A world with no women. . . .''

"What you'd expect," said Grimes. "The really macho types, with their leather and brass, in the armed forces. The effeminate men working as nurses in the creche and other womanly occupations. The in-betweeners were the helots; after all, some-body has to hew the wood and draw the water. But once the bully boys got a whiff of real pussy—*Seeker* had a mixed crew—all hell started to break loose. And there were, too, some women on the planet already. The doctors running the Birth Machine had their own secret harem."

"I expect that you'll find things changed, Commodore," remarked Gunning.

"I shall be surprised if I don't. To begin with, there's no longer a monarchy. The Archon is the boss cocky. And there has been considerable immigration from the Federated Planets—mostly people, as far as I can gather, who have their own ideas about what life was like in Ancient Greece. Billy Williams—who's been acting master of *Sister Sue* during my absence—has been sending me reports."

"That was a nice little time charter you got for your ship," said Gunning. "Earth to Sparta with assorted luxury goods, Spartan spices back. Did your early connections with Sparta help you to get it?"

"Possibly," Grimes told him. He did not add that the Federation Survey Service, in which he still held the reserve captain's commission that not many people knew about, owed him a few favors. He laughed. "But I never thought that *Sister Sue* would be earning her living as a retsina tanker. It's all those immigrants, of course. They must have *real* Greek wine—although the local tipple wasn't at all bad when I was on Sparta years ago—and olives and feta cheese and all the rest of it."

"But surely," objected Gunning, "the ancient Greeks didn't drink retsina. It was the Turks, when they occupied Greece in more recent times, who tried to cure the wine-bibbing Christians of their addiction to alcohol by making them put resin in the wine casks."

"True, true. But you must have found, Captain, that any attempt to revive an ancient culture on a new world is as phony as all hell. The aggressive Scottishness of the Waverley planets, for example. And New Zion—have you ever been there?—where all hands drop whatever they're doing at the drop of a yarmulke to dance the hora. . . . The original culture of the all-male Sparta was phony enough—but it *was* consistent. But now? Unfortunately Billy Williams isn't a very good letter writer but I've gained the impression that those new colonists have succeeded in reproducing an ancient Greece that never was, that never could have been."

"You'll have time to find out for yourself, Commodore. You told me that you'll have about three weeks there before your ship drops in. Unluckily I've only two days' work there—just a small parcel of bagged flour to discharge and a consignment of spices to load—and then I shall be on my way."

The sonorous notes of the dinner gong drifted through the ship.

The two men finished their drinks and got up from their chairs to go down to the dining saloon.

Chapter 3

Grimes quite enjoyed the voyage.

Rim Wayfarer was a comfortable, well-run ship, her captain and officers good company. The food was good, even by Grimes' exacting standards. He was, he admitted to himself, rather surprised. Rim Runners were looked down upon by the personnel of such shipping lines as the Interstellar Transport Commission and Trans-Galactic Clippers and, too, by the officers of the Federation Survey Service. They were the sort of outfit that you joined when nobody else would have you.

But, thought Grimes, *you could do very much worse for yourself.*

The day came when the star tramp dropped from the warped dimensions engendered by her Mannschenn Drive into normal Space-Time. It was a good planetfall, with no more than twelve hours' running under inertial drive to bring the ship to Port Sparta.

Grimes was in the control room, keeping well out of the way, when Gunning made his landing. As far as he could see from the viewports and in the screen everything was much as he remembered it. There, on the hilltop, was the Acropolis, gleaming whitely in the rays of the morning sun. Sprawling around the low mountain was the city, laid out with no regard to geometrical planning, a maze of roads and alleys running between buildings great and small, none of them more than two stories high but some of them covering considerable acreage. Yes, there was the Palace. . . . Grimes supposed that Brasidus, as Archon, would be making it his residence. (The Spartan royal house had ceased to be after the revolution.)

And there was the spaceport. A real spaceport now, capable of handling at least twelve ships at a time. And what ships were in? Obligingly, Gunning's Chief Officer gave Grimes the use of a screen showing the area toward which *Rim Wayfarer* was making her approach. There was something big. Grimes stepped up the magnification. A Trans-Galactic clipper, probably a cruise liner. And something small, but not too small. One of the Survey Service's couriers, Lizard Class. An Epsilon Class tramp—but it couldn't be *Sister Sue*. She, as far as Grimes had been able to determine, must now be about halfway from Earth to Sparta.

Slowly, but not too slowly, *Rim Wayfarer* dropped to her berth, marked by the three scarlet flasher beacons. As always the Port Captain, like Port Captains throughout the Galaxy, had done his best to make the job an awkward one. With all the apron space there was to play with he still expected Gunning to set his ship down between the big cruise liner and the little courier. Luckily there was very little surface wind. The tramp master cursed good naturedly, as Grimes himself, in similar circumstances, had often cursed. He said to Grimes, "Fantastic, isn't it, Commodore? When a man is actually serving as a spaceman he will be a prince of good fellows. Once he takes up ground employment, as a stevedore or a Port Captain or whatever, he has absolutely no consideration for those who used to be his shipmates.... ."

Grimes said, "I was a Port Captain myself once. On Botany Bay."

"And did *you* berth all the ships in a tight huddle so as to leave hectares of great open spaces?"

"I didn't have hectares of great open spaces to play with. Luckily only on one occasion did I have more than one ship in. And then one of them was a relatively small destroyer and the other a really small private yacht."

"So you were the exception to prove the rule," laughed Gunning.

He returned his attention to the controls and the *Wayfarer* dropped steadily down to a neat landing in the exact center of the triangle marked by the flashing beacons.

The port officials boarded.

Grimes remained in his quarters until Gunning buzzed him on the inter-ship telephone, asking him to join him and his official guests in his day cabin. He collected his passport and immunization certificates and made his way up to the captain's flat by the spiral staircase.

There were three visitors in Gunning's office. The captain was sitting behind his paper-strewn desk. Sitting in chairs arranged to face the shipmaster were two men and a woman. One of the men—a customs officer?—was in a kilted uniform that was all leather and brass and a plumed brass helmet was on the deck beside him. At least, thought Grimes, customs officers on this planet did not wear uniforms aping those of honest spacemen. The other man—tall, bald-headed—was wearing a dignified, long white robe. The woman, her back to Grimes, was attired in a simple green tunic that left her suntanned arms and most of her shoulders bare. Her hair, braided and coiled around her head, was a gleaming auburn with the merest touch of gold. There was, thought Grimes, something familiar about her.

"Ah, it's you, Commodore," said Gunning, looking up from the documents. "I thought that it was Melissa with the coffee. . . . But we'll get the introductions over before she brings it in."

The two men and the woman got to their feet, turned to face Grimes.

"Maggie!" he gasped.

"John," she said. (She was not surprised.)

He said, "It's been a long time. . . ."

She said, "It's not all that long since I got you out of that mess aboard *Bronson Star*."

"I mean," said Grimes, "that it's a long time since we were here, on this world, together."

Looking at her he thought, *But she still looks the same as she did then. The face still as beautiful in its high-cheekboned, wide-mouthed way, the figure, revealed rather than concealed by the short, flimsy dress, still as graceful. . . .*

"A long time . . ." he repeated.

"I suppose that it is, at that," she said matter-of-factly. "And here am I, still holding the exalted rank of commander in the Scientific Branch of the Survey Service, and here's you, who've been a yachtmaster, an owner-master, a pirate commodore, a planetary governor and the Odd Gods of the Galaxy alone know what else."

"A privateer," said Grimes. "Not a pirate."

"Whatever you were," she told him, "it's good to see you again."

He took her extended hand, grasped it firmly. He would have kissed her—she seemed to be expecting it—if Gunning had not coughed loudly.

"You already know Commander Lazenby," said the captain. "But may I introduce Colonel Heraclion, Chief Collector of Customs, and Dr. Androcles, Port Health Officer?"

Hands were shaken. Grimes took a chair next to Maggie. The ship's catering officer brought in a tray laden with a large coffee pot, sugar bowl, cream jug and cups. She departed and Gunning poured for his guests.

The colonel said, "I do not usually attend to such matters as the Inward Clearance of shipping myself. But I bear greetings from the Archon." From the leather pouch at his belt he withdrew a large envelope, handed it to Grimes. "To you, sir."

Grimes took it. It was, he noted, unsealed. He remembered having read somewhere that a gentleman, entrusting a letter to another gentleman for delivery, never seals the envelope. Did the ancient Spartans observe such a custom? (Did the ancient Spartans use envelopes?)

He pulled out the sheet of paper—it was more of a card, really. He read the stiff, unfamiliar calligraphy. *The Archon presents his compliments to His Excellency the Commodore Grimes and requests that he will accept the hospitality of the palace during his stay on New Sparta.* It was signed, simply, *Brasidus.*

Grimes passed the card to Maggie.

"Good," she said. "He told me that he would invite you."

"Are you staying there?" he asked.

"Of course." She laughed. "After all, Brasidus and I are old friends. I could be staying aboard *Krait*, of course, but, as you should know, Serpent Class couriers are not famous for their luxurious passenger accommodation."

"So you're here on Survey Service business," remarked Grimes.

"Of course. I'd not have gotten passage here—even if it is in a space-borne sardine can like *Krait*—otherwise. Research. A study of the effects on a Lost Colony by its assimilation into mainstream Galactic culture. Or of the effects on mainstream culture when assimilated into a Lost Colony. Nothing serious, and all good, clean (for most of the time) fun. Perhaps you'd like to help me in my research. That ship of yours isn't due in for some time yet."

"It should be interesting," said Grimes. "But haven't you already found that New Sparta has been spoiled by contact with the rest of the Galaxy?"

"Far from it," she told him. "Anything would have been an improvement on the way it was."

"That," said Colonel Heraclion stiffly, "is your opinion, Commander Lazenby."

Grimes looked at the man with interest. *Yes,* he thought, *there are men to whom an all-male society, such as New Sparta had been, would be almost a paradise. Oh, well. One man's Mede is another man's Persian.*

"I am in agreement with Commander Lazenby," said Dr. Androcles. "Like the colonel, I was a young man when Commodore Grimes' ship, *Seeker,* gave us our first real contact with the outside universe. The people realized then that, for generations, they had been living a lie."

"In the opinion of your medical profession, perhaps," sneered the colonel. "But do not forget that you and your colleagues had been promulgating that same lie."

"Gentlemen, gentlemen," chided Captain Gunning. "I do not think that my day cabin is a fitting venue for a heated argument about New Spartan politics."

"It was the outworlders who started it," said Heraclion sourly.

"Outworlders," Maggie reminded him, "who just happen to be honored guests of your Archon."

The colonel was about to make a heated reply, then thought better of it. Dr. Androcles laughed.

"I'll help you to finish your packing, John," said Maggie.

Chapter 4

When they were alone in his quarters Grimes kissed her. She returned his embrace, then pushed him away.

"Not now," she said. "There'll be plenty of time for this sort of thing in the palace."

"Will there?" he asked. "Haven't you already said that you and the Archon are old friends? I . . . assumed. . . ."

"Then you assumed wrong. Ellena keeps Brasidus on a tight leash."

"Ellena?"

"His wife. The Archoness, as many call her, although there's no such rank or title. She's from Earth. An Australian, of Greek ancestry. Very much the power behind the throne. But finish your packing and I'll fill you in." She took from its shelf the solidograph that she had given him—how long ago?—and held the transparent cube, with its lifelike, three dimensional image of her face and figure, studying it before passing it to him. "You're something of a sentimental bastard, aren't you? That's one of the reasons why I'm rather fond of you."

"Thank you."

"And now for putting you in the picture. To begin with, my research project is only a cover. I was seconded to the Intelligence Branch, and by them put under the orders of Rear Admiral Damien."

"But he's not in the Intelligence Branch."

"Isn't he? There are intelligence officers whom everybody knows about and there are intelligence officers who, as it were, hide their light under a bushel. Like you, for example."

"Me?"

"Yes, you. The admiral told me that you had been pressganged back into the Survey Service with the rank of captain on the Reserve List. All very Top Secret, Destroy By Fire Before Reading and all the rest of it. What you did to break up Drongo Kane's privateering racket was no more—and no less—than Intelligence work. So was what you did on Liberia. Whether you knew it or not you were a member of the Department of Dirty Tricks."

Grimes sighed. "All right, all right. But just what dirty tricks am I supposed to be doing here?"

"Just shoving a spanner into the works."

"But Brasidus—from what I remember of him—is a nice enough bloke. I'm sure that he's a good Archon, whatever an Archon does when he's up and dressed. There's never been any talk of tyranny, so far as I know. People are still emigrating to New Sparta from Earth and other planets."

She said, "That's part of the trouble."

"How so?"

"One of our people was among those migrants. Under cover, of course. According to her papers she was a schoolteacher. She sent a few reports back to Earth—and then they stopped coming. Since my arrival here I've been able to make discreet inquiries. She was drowned in a boating accident."

"If it was an accident . . ." said Grimes. "Is that what you're driving at?"

"Of course. She was out on a river trip with other members of the New Hellas Association. Colonel Heraclion—although he wasn't a member of the boating party—is one of the Association's high-ups. Oh, I know what you're thinking. *New* Hellas, when what he wants is *Old* New Sparta. But the New Hellenes are a bunch of reactionaries. Some—like the good colonel—want a return to a womanless world, the way it used to be. Others—and they're mainly immigrants—want a return to the way ancient Greece used to be on Earth."

"The glory that was Greece . . ." quoted Grimes. "What's so wrong with that?"

"Ancient Greece," she told him, "was glorious, if you happened to be a member of the upper crust and male. If you were a slave, a peasant or a woman it wasn't so glorious."

"But there are women in this New Hellas Association. This murdered agent of yours—all right, all right, of ours—was a member and a woman."

"There are some women," she said, "who, in their secret hearts, would enjoy being human doormats. There are other women who would enjoy being glamorous *hetaerae* in a society where the other members of their sex were no more than drab *Hausfrauen*."

"*Hetaerae* and *Hausfrauen* in the same culture!" laughed Grimes.

"You know what I mean. Well, it wouldn't be so bad if the New Hellenes were just trying to attain their ends by democratic means but, according to our late agent, they're plotting a coup. A coup on classical lines. And then yet another unsavory dictatorship which, eventually, will have to be put down at great expense. If such things can be nipped in the bud. . . ."

"By whom?"

"Need you ask, ducky?"

"Damn it all," said Grimes, "I'm a civilian. A shipmaster and shipowner. All that I came to this world for was to rejoin my ship."

"You're not a civilian, John. Oh, you may have been for a while, but ever since you accepted that reserve commission you've been back in the Service. I've written orders for you from Admiral Damien—not with me at the moment but in the captain's safe aboard the courier. I'll get them out for you before too long."

The intercom phone buzzed. Grimes pressed the *Acknowledge* button. Gunning's face appeared in the screen.

"I hope that I'm not interrupting anything, Commodore, but Colonel Heraclion asked me to remind you that the car is waiting to take you to the palace. If you like I'll send somebody down to give you a hand with your gear."

"Thank you, Captain," said Grimes. "But don't I have to pass Port Health, Immigration and Customs?"

"The colonel informs me that all formalities have been waived in your case." The master laughed. "It's always handy to have friends in high places."

The screen went blank.

Grimes opened the door of his cabin in preparation for the arrival of the junior officer who would help him with his bags. Maggie continued talking but only on topics which, should she be overheard, would give nobody any ideas.

"Talking of friends," she said, "I met one of yours a couple of days ago."

"But the only person whom I got to know on this world, when I was here before, was Brasidus."

"This one's an offworlder."

"From Earth?"

"No. From Bronsonia. An investigative reporter, she calls herself. She works for that scurrilous rag *Star Scandals*. She's doing a series on sleazy entertainment centers on as many worlds as she can get to visit during the time allowed her. She's tailing along after some outfit calling itself Galactic Glamour, featuring exotic dancers from all over. They're doing a short season here before pushing on to Latterhaven.

"Anyhow, I met her when I was slumming, as part of my research. We had a couple or three drinks. She knew that I'm Survey Service. And you know how stupid people are . . ." She assumed a voice that was not hers but which was ominously familiar to Grimes. *"Oh, you're in the Survey Service . . . A commander. Do you know Commander Smith?"* She laughed. "What she said was, *Do you know Captain Grimes? He used to be in the Survey Service—he got as high as commander, I believe, before they threw him out . . ."*

"I resigned!" growled Grimes.

"So I said to her, *Who doesn't know Grimes?* And she grinned nastily and said, *So we share that dubious pleasure.* But don't you want to know who she is?"

"I know only one person who answers to your description of her," muttered Grimes. "But tell me, is she, too, a guest at the palace?"

"No. She did come calling around once, flashing her press ID, but Ellena took an instant dislike to her. The guards have strict orders never to admit her again."

"Thank All The Odd Gods Of The Galaxy for that! With any luck at all I'll not be meeting her again."

"Then your luck's run out. You surely don't think, do you, that you'll be confined to the palace during your entire stay here? Apart from anything else you'll be helping me with my ethnographical research—and I've little doubt that our path will, from time to time, cross that of the fair researcher for *Star Scandals*."

"I don't frequent low joints," said Grimes virtuously.

"Then you've changed!" she laughed.

He laughed with her. "Oh, well, I shan't really mind meeting Fenella again for a talk over old times. But it's a pity that Shirl and Darleen aren't here as well . . ."

"And who are they?" asked Maggie, with a touch of jealousy.

"Just girls," said Grimes.

And then the Third Officer appeared to help carry the baggage down to the airlock.

Chapter 5

At the foot of the ramp two of Heraclion's men loaded Grimes' baggage into the rear of the hovercar—a vehicle that was doing its best to look like an ancient Greek chariot—while the commodore said his farewells to Captain Gunning and the star tramp's officers. The colonel took his seat alongside the driver who, like his superior, was dressed in brass and leather although with much less of the glittering metal on display. Maggie and Grimes sat immediately behind the two Spartans.

The ducted fans whined loudly and raised eddies of dust. The vehicle lifted itself in its skirts, slid away from the spaceship, picking up speed as it did so. Soon it was clear of the spaceport environs, proceeding at a good rate toward the city. There was other vehicular traffic—chariotlike hovercraft, both military and civil, carts piled with produce and drawn by what looked like donkeys and mules, imports from distant Earth. There were, as there had been on the occasion of Grimes' previous visit, squads of young men, who appeared to be soldiers, on motorcycles but there were others on horseback.

Grimes remarked on what was, to him, archaic means of transport.

Heraclion, speaking back over his shoulder, said, "There are those among our new citizens, Commodore, who want to put the clock back to the time of the Spartan Empire on Earth. . . ." (*The Spartan Empire?* wondered Grimes. He most certainly could not recall any mention of such during his studies of Terran history.) "Even so, I have to admit that a troop of cavalry mounted on horseback is a far better spectacle than one mounted on motorcycles."

The hovercar, its siren screaming to demand right of way, was now fast approaching the outskirts of the city. It sped along the narrow road between the rows of low, white houses and less privileged traffic hastily made way for it. A turn was made into what was little more than a winding lane. This, Grimes realized, must be the entertainment district. In the old days, during his first visit to Sparta, such a venue was undreamed of. Gaudy neon signs, dim on the sunny side of the street but bright in the shadow, advertised the delights available to those with money behind the heavy wooden doors, the shuttered windows. The lettering, although aping the Cyrillic alphabet, spelled out its messages in Standard English.

DIMITRIO'S LAMB BARBECUE—TOPLESS LADY CHEFS
(Grimes could appreciate the female cooks' need for aprons; barbecues are apt to sputter and spatter.)
HELEN'S HETAERAE
(And did one drop in there for intellectual conversation?)
ARISTOTLE'S ARENA
This was a much larger building than the rest. Under the flickering main sign were others:

GALACTIC GLAMOUR
EXOTIC WARRIOR MAIDS
OFFPLANET AMAZONS
LIMITED SEASON ONLY

Maggie had to put her mouth to his ear to be heard above the shrieking siren. "That's the outfit I was telling you about. The one that your old girlfriend is doing the series on." She laughed. "The trouble with Aristotle is that he's not a very good historian. His entertainment is more Roman than Grecian. I think that he'd even put on Lions versus Christians if he thought he could get away with it."

"Have you been there?"

"Yes. That's where I met Fenella Pruin. After I admitted that I knew you she laughed nastily and said, 'This is just the sort of show that he'd enjoy. A pity he's not here.' I didn't tell her, of course, that you were on your way to Sparta."

"Thank you. With only a little bit of luck she'll never know I'm here."

"She'll know all right. The local media have already bruited abroad that the famous Commodore John Grimes is to be the guest of the Archon."

"Then I'll just have to rely on you to keep her out of my hair."

They were out of the Street of the Haetaeri as the red-light district was called, making the ascent of the low hill on top of which stood the Archon's palace. Troops were drawn up before the long, pillared portico, weapons and accouterments gleaming in the afternoon sunlight. Short spears were raised in salute as the hovercar whined to a stop and subsided to the ground.

Grimes looked at the soldiers appreciatively. They were young women, all of them, uniformed in short white tunics and heavy, brass-studded sandals with knee-high lacings. The leather cross-straps and belts defined their breasts and hips sharply. Shoulder length hair, in almost every case glossily blonde, flowed from under their plumed helmets.

"The Lady Ellena's Amazon Guard," commented Heraclion sourly.

"I'd sooner have them than a bunch of hairy-arsed Federation Marines," said Grimes.

Maggie's elbow dug sharply into his ribs.

They disembarked then—Maggie, Grimes and the colonel.

The Amazon officer marched before them, her spear held high. Other girls fell in on either side of them, escorting them. They passed through the great doorway into the hall, dim after the blazing sunlight outside, to where the Archon and his lady, flanked by berobed dignitaries of both sexes, awaited them.

Grimes found it hard to recognize Brasidus. The young, clean-shaven sergeant whom he had known was now a portly, middle-aged man, his hair and full beard touched with gray. Perhaps it was the white robe with its broad purple trim that gave an illusion of stoutness but the commodore did not think so. Brasidus would never have been able to buckle on the simple uniform that he had worn in the old days.

And the large woman who stood beside the Archon was indubitably stout. She, too, wore a purple-trimmed robe. Her rather spuriously golden hair was piled high and elaborately upon her head but even without this added height she would have been at least fifteen centimeters taller than her husband. She looked down her long nose at the guests with very cold blue eyes and her full mouth was set in a disapproving line.

The Amazon guard grounded their spears with an echoing crash.

Brasidus stepped forward, both hands extended.

Grimes had started to bow but realized that this salutation would not be correct. He straightened up and extended his own right hand. The Archon grasped it warmly in both of his.

"John Grimes! It is indeed good to see you again, after all these years! My house is yours while you are on Sparta!"

"Thank you . . . Lord," said Grimes.

"And have you forgotten my name? To my friends I am, and always will be, just Brasidus. But allow me to present my lady wife. Ellena, my dear, this is John Grimes, of whom you have often heard. . . ."

"The famous pirate commodore," said the woman in neutral tones.

"And John, this is the Lady Ellena."

She extended a large, plump hand with scarlet fingernails. Grimes somehow got the impression that he was to do no more than touch it. He did that.

There were other introductions, to each of the assembled councilmen and councilwomen. There was an adjournment to a large room where refreshments were served by girls who circulated among the guests pouring the wine—a Terran retsina, Grimes decided, although he thought that it had not traveled well—from long necked *amphorae*. There were feta cheese and black olives (imported?) to nibble.

Finally the party broke up and Grimes was escorted to his quarters by one of the servant wenches. They could have been a hotel suite on just about any planet.

He was sitting down for a quiet smoke when Maggie joined him.

"Dinner's at 1900 hours," she told him. "No need to get out your penguin suit or a dress uniform. It'll be just a small occasion with Brasidus, you and me reminiscing over old times."

"What about the Lady Ellena?"

"She's off to a meeting. She's Patron of the Women's Branch of the New Hellas Association."

"But . . ." He hesitated. "Is it all right to talk?"

"It is. I was supplied with the very latest thing in bug detectors. When it's not detecting bugs it functions quite well as a wristwatch."

"What about Ellena and the New Hellas mob?"

"I don't think she's mixed up in any of their subversive activities. She's a silly bitch, but not that silly. She knows which side her bread is buttered. But she loves being fawned upon and flattered.''

"I take it she's of relatively humble origins.''

"Correct. She was an assistant in a ladies' hairdressing salon in Melbourne, Australia. She was proud of her Greek ancestry. When New Sparta was thrown open to immigration from Earth she scraped together her savings and borrowed quite a few credits—which she repaid, by the way; I give her credit for that—with the idea of setting up in the same line of business here, getting in on the ground floor. Of course, in the beginning ladies' hairdressers were something of a novelty and quite a few men wandered into them by mistake to get their flowing locks trimmed and their beards curled. Brasidus made that mistake. He didn't know much about women then and she knew who he was—he wasn't yet Archon but he was on the way up—and poured on the motherly charm. She was able to hitch her wagon to his rising star.''

"So Cinderella married the handsome prince,'' said Grimes sardonically. "And they all lived happily ever after.''

She said, "We have some living to do ourselves after all this time.''

She led the way into his bedroom.

Chapter 6

It had been a long time, as she had said, but after the initial fumbling there was the old, sweet familiarity, the fitting of part to part, the teasing caress of hands on skin, of lips on lips and then, from her, the sharp yet melodious cries as he drove deeper and deeper and his own groans as her arms and legs imprisoned his body, her heels pummeling his buttocks.

They did not—they were out of practice with each other—reach climax together but her orgasm preceded his by only a few seconds.

They would rather have remained in the rumpled bed, to talk

lazily for a while and then, after not too long an interval, to resume their love-making but, after all, they were guests and, furthermore, guests in the palace of a planetary ruler. Such people, no matter how humble their origins (or, perhaps, especially if their origins were humble) do not care to be kept waiting. So they showered together—but did not make an erotic game of it—and resumed their clothing. Maggie, who, by this time, was well acquainted with the layout of the palace, led Grimes to the small, private dining room where they were to eat with the Archon. They arrived there just before Brasidus.

The meal was a simple one, served by two very homely maidservants. There was a sort of casserole of some meat that might have been lamb, very heavily spiced. There was a rough red wine that went surprisingly well with the main course. For a sweet there was not too bad baclava, accompanied by thick, syrupy coffee. "We do not grow our own yet," said Brasidus, "but we hope to be doing so by next year. Soon, John, there will be no need for your *Sister Sue* to bring us cargoes of such luxuries from Earth." He laughed. "And what will you do then to make an honest living? Return to a career of piracy or find another governor's job?" There was brandy, in warmed inhalers, a quite good Metaxa.

The serving wenches cleared away the debris of the meal.

Having asked the permission of their host Grimes lit his pipe and Maggie a cigarillo. They were expecting, both of them, to settle down to an evening of reminiscent conversation over the brandy bottle but Brasidus surprised them.

"Help yourselves to more drinks, if you wish," he told them. "I am going to change. I shall not keep you long."

"To change, Brasidus?" asked Grimes.

"Yes. I have heard much of that new show at the Arena— you, Maggie, told me of it. I have not seen it yet. Ellena does not approve of such entertainment. I thought that this evening would be an ideal opportunity for me to witness the . . . the goings on."

"You're the boss," said Grimes.

When he was gone Maggie said, "He likes doing the Haroun al-Raschid thing now and again. Strolling among his citizens incognito, keeping his finger on the pulse and all the rest of it. Ellena doesn't altogether approve, but when the cat's away. . . ."

"And we're among the mice this evening, I suppose."

"I'm afraid so. But *you* should enjoy the show at the Arena. As I recall you, you have a thing about the weirder variations of the female face and form divine. That cat woman on Morrowvia with whom you had a roll in the hay. That *peculiar* clone or whatever she was from whom the Survey Service had to rescue you when you were trying to get *Bronson Star* back to where she had been skyjacked from. There have been others, no doubt.''

"Mphm," grunted Grimes through a cloud of acrid tobacco smoke. He refilled the brandy inhalers. "Mphm."

"I will have one too," said Brasidus.

Grimes stared at him. Had it not been for the man's voice he would never have recognized the Archon. Yet the disguise was simple enough, just a spray-on dye applied to hair and beard, converting what had been light brown hair with the occasional silver thread to a not unnatural looking black.

The Archon drained his glass, then led the way out of the small dining room.

They made their way to what Grimes thought of as the tradesmen's entrance.

Two men were waiting for them there, dressed, as was Grimes, in one-piece gray suits in a somewhat outmoded Terran style. Unlike Grimes, who liked a touch of garish color in his neckwear, they had on cravats that almost exactly matched the color and texture of the rest of their clothing. Their side pockets bulged, as did Grimes'. Were they, he wondered, also pipe smokers? The Archon himself was dressed in the clothing appropriate to a lower middle class citizen on a night out—knee-length blue tunic with touches of golden embroidery, rather elaborate sandals with, it seemed, more brass (not very well polished) than leather. Maggie had on the modified Greek female dress that had been introduced from Earth—a short, white, rather flimsy tunic, sleeveless and with one of her shoulders left completely bare.

Brasidus introduced his two bodyguards—or so Grimes thought they must be; they looked the part—as Jason and Paulus. They could have been twins—although, he found later, they were not even related. They were tallish rather than tall, stoutish rather than stout and wore identical sullen expressions on their utterly undistinguished faces.

Jason brought a rather battered four-passenger hovercar round to the portico. It looked like something bought, cheaply, from Army Surplus. But there was nothing at all wrong with its engine and Grimes noticed various bulges in its exterior paneling that probably concealed weapons of some kind.

Jason was a good driver.

Soon the vehicle was whining through the narrow streets of the city which, mainly, were illuminated by deliberately archaic gas flares, avoiding near collisions with contemptuous ease, finally gliding into the garish neon glare of the Street of the Haetaeri. Parking was found very close to the entrance of Aristotle's Arena. The three men and the woman got out and walked the short distance to the ticket booth. Brasidus pulled a clinking coin purse from the pouch at his belt and paid admission for the party.

"It's a good show, citizen," said the ticket vendor, a woman who was disguised as a Japanese geisha but whose face, despite the thickly applied cosmetics, was more Caucasian than Asian. "You're just in time to see the cat girls doing their thing."

Maggie, who had been to this place before, led the way down a flight of stone stairs. At the bottom of these they emerged from dim lighting into what was almost complete darkness. An usherette dressed in what looked like an imitation of an Amazon guard's uniform—but the tip of her short spear functioned as a torch—led them to their seats, which were four rows back from the circular, sand-covered arena. She sold them doughnut-shaped pneumatic cushions—the seating was on stone benches—which they had to inflate themselves. As they settled down in an approximation to comfort the show started.

There was music of some kind over the public address system. Grimes didn't recognize the tune. Maggie whispered, "But you should, John. Apparently it's a song that was popular on Earth—oh, centuries ago. Somebody must have done his homework. It's called, 'What's new, Pussycat?' "

Brasidus muttered sourly, "Some Earth imports we could do without."

A spotlight came on, illuminating the thing that emerged from the tunnel that gave entrance to the arena. It was . . . *Surely not!* thought Grimes. But it was. It was a giant mouse. A robot mouse, its movements almost lifelike. There were no real mice on New Sparta, of course, although immigrants from Earth knew about them and there were now plenty of illustrated books on Terran zoology. And cats, real cats, had been introduced by the Terran immigrants.

The mouse made an unsteady circuit of the arena.

Two more spotlights came on, shining directly onto the naked bodies of the two Morrowvian dancers. Their makeup accentuated their feline appearance, striped body paint making them look like humanoid tigresses. Spiky, artificial whiskers decorated their cheeks and vicious fangs protruded from their mouths.

They did not make the mistake of dropping to all fours but they moved with catlike grace, in time to the wailing music.

They stalked the mouse from opposite directions and whoever was at the remote controls of the robot managed to convey a quite convincing impression of animal panic, even to a thin, high, terrified squeaking. Every now and again one of the girls would catch it, but do no more than stoop gracefully to bat the robot off its feet with a swipe of a pawlike hand. Each time it recovered and made another dash, and then the other girl would deal with it as her companion had done.

Finally the audience was tiring of the cat and mouse game. There were shouts of, "Finish it! Finish it!"

The taller of the two girls pounced. She dropped to her knees and brought her mouth, with those vicious fangs, down to the neck of the giant mouse. There was a final, ear-piercing squeak. There must have been bladders full of some red fluid under the robot's synthetic skin; a jet of what looked like blood spurted out over the cat woman's face, dripped on to the sand. She made her exit then, still on all fours, the carcass hanging from her mouth. Either the robot was very light or those false teeth were very securely anchored.

Her companion trailed after her, also on her hands and knees, caterwauling jealously.

The applause could have been more enthusiastic but, even so, the audience wasn't sitting on its collective hands.

"Quite good," admitted Brasidus. Then, "You have been to Morrowvia, John and Maggie. Do the people there really hunt like that?"

"They are fond of hunting," Maggie told him. "But they hunt much larger animals than mice, and they use spears and bows and arrows. And their teeth, after all the engineered genetic alterations, are like yours and mine. And they don't have whiskers. And their skins aren't striped, although their hair, on the head and elsewhere, often is. . . ."

"Please leave me some illusions," laughed Brasidus.

But Grimes was not listening to them.

He was looking across the arena to where a tangle of audio and video recording equipment had been set up. In the middle of this, like a malignant female spider in her web, was a woman.

Even over a distance Grimes recognized her, and thereafter, while the lights were still on, tried to keep his face turned away from her. Eating one of the hot, spiced sausages that Brasidus had bought from a passing attendant helped.

Chapter 7

"Citizens!" The voice of the master of ceremonies blared from the public address system. "Citizens! Now it is my great pleasure to announce the two boxing kangaroos from New Alice . . ." There was an outburst of applause; obviously this was a very popular act. Grimes could not catch the names of the performers. It would be too much of a coincidence, he thought, if they should turn out to be Shirl and Darleen. Those ladies had been in show business on New Venusberg but as quarry in the so-called kangaroo hunt. He knew that they could fight—first as gladiators in the Colosseum and then helping to beat off a Shaara attack—but their weapons had been boomerangs, not their fists. "And now may I call for volunteers? You know the rules. No weapons, bare fists only. Should any one of you succeed in knocking down one of the ladies she will be yours for the night. Stand up, those who wish to take part in the prize fight of the century! The usherettes will escort you to the changing room."

All around the arena men were getting to their feet. There was no shortage of volunteers.

"What about you, John?" asked Maggie. "Wouldn't you like to add a New Alician to your list of conquests?"

"No," Grimes said. "No." (He had no need to tell her that he and those two New Alicians, Shirl and Darleen, had been rather more than just good friends.)

"*I* am tempted," said Brasidus.

"It would not be wise," said Jason.

The last of the volunteers—there had been two dozen of them—had been led to the changing room. The house lights dimmed. There was taped music, an old Australian folk song that Grimes recognized. *Tie me kangaroo down, sport, tie me kangaroo down* . . . Some, more than a few, of the audience, knew the words and started to sing. Grimes joined them.

"Please don't," said Maggie, wincing exaggeratedly.

29

Then the song was over and the music that replaced it was old, old. There was the eerie whispering of the didgerydoo, the xylophonic clicking of singing sticks. Out of the tunnel and onto the sand bounded the two New Alicians, their hands held like paws in front of their small breasts. Save for the absence of long, muscular tails they could well have been large, albino kangaroos. As they hopped around the ring the lights over the arena itself brightened and some, but not all, of the illusion evaporated. But it was still obvious that the remote ancestry of these girls had not been human. There were the heavy rumps, the very well-developed thighs, the lower legs inclined to be skinny, something odd about the jointure of the knees. They were horse-faced, but pleasantly so, handsome rather than pretty, not quite beautiful. They were. . . .

Surely not! thought Grimes. This would be altogether too much of a coincidence. First Maggie (but his and her presence on this world together was perhaps not so coincidental), then Fenella Pruin, and now Shirl and Darleen. But he knew, all too well, that real life abounds in coincidences that a fiction writer would never dare to introduce.

The music fell silent. There was a roll of drums, a blaring trumpet. There was the voice of the announcer as the first pair of volunteers, in bright scarlet boxer shorts, came trotting out through the tunnel.

"Citizens! Killer Kronos and Battling Bellepheron, to uphold the honor of New Sparta!"

The men, both of them heavily muscled louts, raised their fists above their heads and turned slowly to favor each and every member of the audience with simian grins.

A bell sounded.

The men advanced upon their female adversaries, clenched fists ready to deliver incapacitating blows. Shirl and Darleen stood their ground. Kronos launched what should have been a devastating swipe, that would have been one such had it connected. But Shirl little more than shrugged and the fist missed her left ear by considerably more than the thickness of a coat of paint. And then she was on him, her own fists pummeling his chest and belly. He roared with rage and tried to throw his thick arms about her, to crush her into submission. She danced back and he embraced nothingness. What happened next was almost too fast for the eye to follow. She jumped straight up and drove both feet into his midsection. It was almost as though she were balanced on a stout, muscular but invisible tail. She and Kronos hit the sand simultaneously, she in a crouching posture, he flat on his back. He stirred feebly, made an attempt to get up and then slumped.

Meanwhile Darleen was disposing of her own adversary by more orthodox means, using fists only. It was a classical knock-out.

So it went on. Some bouts were ludicrously short, others gave better value for the customers' money. Some challengers limped out of the arena under their own steam, others had to be carried off.

Brasidus was highly amused. "These wenches," he said, "would make a better showing in a fight than the Lady Ellena's Amazon Guards. But I suppose that unarmed combat is all that they're good at."

"Not so," said Grimes. "Their real specialty is throwing weapons. With them they're lethal."

"You seem to know a lot about the people of New Alice," Maggie said. "Have you ever been there?"

"No," he told her. "I . . . I met some of them once, on another planet." (Perhaps some day he would tell her of his misadventures on New Venusberg. Had it not been for the inhibiting influence of Eldoradan investors in the more dubious entertainments available on the pleasure planet the galactic media would have given him and Fenella Pruin more than their fair share of notoriety. As it was, hardly anybody knew what had happened and the part that Grimes had played.)

"Javelins?" asked Brasidus, his mind still on weaponry.

"Not quite. For throwing spears they use something called a *woomera*, a throwing stick, which they use like a sling. It gives the spears extra range. But their most spectacular weapon is the boomerang. . . ."

"And what is that, John?"

Before Grimes could reply the voice of the announcer boomed over the auditorium.

"And now, citizens, the two wonder women from New Alice, the splendiferous Shirl and the delicious Darleen, will entertain you with an exhibition of the art of boomerang throwing. The boomerang is a weapon developed on their native world in Stone Age days, millennia before there were such things as computers and yet employing and utilizing the most subtle principles of modern aerodynamics. . . ."

"The boomerang was developed on Earth, long before New Alice was ever dreamed of," whispered Grimes indignantly.

All the lights came on and the auditorium was now as brightly illumined as the arena itself. Shirl and Darleen stood in the center of the ring, their naked bodies gleaming in the harsh glare. Despite their participation in twelve boxing bouts their skins were unmarked. Slowly they scanned the audience. At one time Grimes thought they were looking straight at him but they gave no sign of recognition. But, of course, they would not be expecting to see him here. After the show he would go around to the stage door, or whatever it was called, to give the girls a big surprise.

Two of the pseudo Amazons came onto the arena, each carrying a small bundle of wooden boomerangs. There were big ones, and some not so big, and little ones. They were decorated with bands of bright paint—white and blue and scarlet.

The attendants bowed to Shirl and Darleen and then strode away. There was the obligatory roll of drums. Shirl picked up a half dozen of the little boomerangs from the sand. She handed the first one to Darleen, who threw it from her. Then the second one, then the third, then the fourth, and the fifth and the sixth. It was a dazzling display of juggling with never less than five of the things in the air at the same time, each one terminating its short, circular flight in Darleen's right hand just after the launching of another, resting there only briefly before being relaunched itself. And then the flight pattern was changed and it was Shirl who was catching, one by one, all six of the boomerangs, catching and throwing time after time again. Another half dozen of the boomerangs came into play and Shirl and Darleen widened the distance between themselves, a boomerang-juggling duo.

Finally each of the things was thrown so that they came to rest in the center of the arena, forming a pile that could not have been neater had it been stacked by hand.

There was the big boomerang flung by Shirl (or was it Darleen? Grimes still had trouble distinguishing one from the other) that made several orbits of the main overhead light, like a misshapen planet about its primary, before returning to its thrower's hand. There were the medium-sized ones that were sent whirling over the heads of the audience, too high for any rash person to try to catch one at the risk of losing a finger or two. Most of these were directed to the vicinity of where Fenella Pruin was sitting amidst her recording apparatus.

At last the girls decided that they had given her enough of a show and turned to face that part of the auditorium where the Archon's party was sitting. They scanned the faces of the audience and then they were looking directly at Grimes. They held a whispered consultation, then looked at him again. So they had recognized him. So he would not be able to surprise them in their dressing room when the show was over. It was rather a pity. He shrugged.

Shirl (or was it Darleen?) picked up one of the medium-sized boomerangs. She looked at Grimes. He looked at her. He raised a hand in a gesture of greeting. Both girls ignored it. Shirl assumed the thrower's stance. Her right arm was a blur of motion—and then the boomerang was coming straight at Grimes, the rapidity of its rotation about its short axis making it almost invisible. He tried to duck but he was jammed in between Maggie and Jason and unable to move.

There was a sudden rattle of automatic pistol fire; Paulus had pulled his vicious little Minetti from a side pocket. The boomerang disintegrated in mid-flight, its shredded splinters falling harmlessly onto the people in the front row. There were shouts and screams. There were two of the pseudo-Amazon usherettes making their hasty way to the scene of the disturbance—and they were not so pseudo after all; each was holding a pistol, a stungun but a weapon nonetheless and lethal when set to full intensity. Jason had his pistol out now and he and the other bodyguard were both standing, pointing their Minettis at the approaching Amazons.

"Put them down, you fools!" roared Brasidus.

Grimes hoped that they would have enough sense to realize that he meant the guns, not the chuckers-out.

The stunguns buzzed. They had been set at very low intensity, not even causing temporary paralysis but inducing a dazed grogginess. The two Amazons were joined by four more strapping, uniformed wenches and the Archon's party was dragged ignominiously to the manager's office.

Ironic applause accompanied their forced departure from the auditorium.

Chapter 8

Aristotle was a fat man, bald, piggy eyed, clad in a white robe similar to those worn by the professional classes, soiled down the front by dropped cigar ash and liquor spillage. He was smoking a cigar now, speaking around it as he addressed the prisoners who stood before his wide, littered desk, supported by the Amazon usherettes.

"You . . ." he snarled. "You . . . Offworlders by the look of you . . . At an entertainment such as mine some riotous behavior is tolerated, but not riotous behavior with . . . *firearms*." With a pudgy hand he poked disdainfully at the two automatic pistols that had been placed on his desk. "I suppose you'll try to tell me—and the police, when they get here, and the magistrate when you come up for trial—that you didn't know that on this world civilians are not allowed to carry such weapons, by order of the Archon. You know now."

"But this . . ." Jason waved feebly toward Brasidus. "But this is the . . ."

The Archon raised a warning hand, glared at his bodyguard.

"And this is what, or who?" demanded the showman disdainfully. "Some petty tradesman enjoying a night on the tiles with his offplanet friends, at their expense, no doubt. Showing them the sights, as long as they're doing the paying. And, talking of the foreigners, which of them started the gunplay?"

"This one," said the Amazon supporting Paulus, giving him a friendly cuff as she spoke.

"So it was you," growled Aristotle. "And now, sir, would you mind satisfying my curiosity before the police come to collect you? What possessed you to pull a gun in a public place and, even worse, to interrupt a highly skilled act by two of my performers?"

"That . . . That boomerang thing . . . It was coming straight at the Commodore. I did my best to protect him."

34

"The Commodore? You mean the gentleman with the jug handle ears? I do have a distinguished clientele, don't I? I know of only one visiting Commodore on New Sparta at this time, and *he* is a guest of the Archon. He'd be too much of a stuffed shirt to sample the pleasures of the Street of the Haetaeri."

"Little you know," said a familiar female voice.

Aristotle shifted his attention from the prisoners to somebody who had just come into the office. "Oh, Miss Pruin . . ." he said coldly. "I do not think that you were invited to sit in on this interview."

"I invited myself," said Fenella. "After all, news is news."

Grimes managed to turn his head to look at her. She had changed very little, if not at all. Her face with rather too much nose and too little chin, with teeth slightly protuberant, the visage of an insatiably curious animal but perversely attractive nonetheless. She grinned at him.

"Do you know these people?" he demanded.

"Not all of them, Aristotle. But the gentleman with the jug handle ears is Captain Grimes, although I believe that he did, briefly, hold the rank of Company Commodore with the Eldorado Corporation. That was when he commanded a pirate squadron. . . ."

"Privateers," Grimes corrected her tiredly. "Not pirates."

She ignored this. "And the lady is Commander Maggie Lazenby, one of the scientific officers of the Federation Survey Service. Both she and Captain—sorry, Commodore—Grimes were on this planet many years ago and were involved in the troubles that led to the downfall of the old regime."

"Oh. *That* Grimes," said Aristotle. His manner seemed to be softening slightly. "But I still am entitled to an explanation as to why his friend ruined the Shirl and Darleen act."

"The boomerang," insisted Paulus, "was coming straight at the Commodore. It could have taken his head off."

"It would not," said two familiar female voices speaking in chorus. Shirl and Darleen, light robes thrown around their bodies, had come into the office which, although considerably larger than a telephone booth, was getting quite crowded. "It would not."

"It would not," Aristotle agreed. "Surely you know what that part of the act signified?"

"The boomerang," explained Shirl (or was it Darleen?), "would have stopped and turned just short of you, returning to my hand. It was a signal to you that you were to follow it—after the show, of course. I thought that everybody knew."

"It was announced," said Aristotle. "Just as it was announced that any boxer who succeeded in knocking down Shirl or Darleen would be entitled to her favors."

"It was *not* announced," said Grimes.

"It was *not* announced," said Jason and Paulus, speaking together.

"Well, it should have been," admitted Aristotle. "But all of my regular customers know of the arrangement."

"We are not regular customers," said Brasidus.

"But that, sir, does not entitle your friends to brandish and discharge firearms in my auditorium." He raised and turned his head. "Come in, Sergeant, come in! I shall be obliged if you will place these persons under arrest. No, not Commodore Grimes and Commander Lazenby, they are guests of the Archon. But the other three. Charge them with discharging firearms, illegally held firearms at that, in a public place."

"If you would please tell me who is which . . ." said the Sergeant tiredly.

He looked at Grimes. "Oh, I recognize you, sir. Your photograph was in the *Daily Democrat*. But which of the ladies am I supposed to take in?"

He stood there in his military style uniform (but black instead of brown leather, stainless steel instead of brass), removing his plumed helmet so that he could scratch his head. The two constables, reluctant to enter the crowded office, remained outside the now open door.

"Just the men, Sergeant," Aristotle told him impatiently. "Just the men."

"All right." The Sergeant grabbed Brasidus by the arm that was not held by an Amazon usherette. "Come on, you. Come quietly, or else."

"But that is the Archon," objected Paulus in a shocked voice. He tried to break away from restraint so that he could come to his master's aid. "Take your paws off the Archon!"

"And I'm Zeus masquerading as a mere mortal!" The Sergeant pulled Brasidus towards the door. "Come *on*!"

"He *is* the Archon," stated Grimes.

"Come, come, sir. This lout is nothing like Brasidus. I did duty in the Palace Guard before the Lady Ellena had us replaced by her Amazon Corps. I've a good memory for details—have to in my job. His hair and beard are light brown, just starting to go gray. Besides—" he laughed—"Ellena would never allow him to come to a dive like this."

"My establishment is not a dive!" expostulated Aristotle indignantly.

"Isn't it? Then what's it doing on *this* street?" He called to the constables. "Come in, you two, and grab the other two lawbreakers."

"There'll be some room for us after you get out," muttered one of the men.

The Sergeant twisted Brasidus' right arm behind his back. It must have been painful.

"Take your hands off me!" growled Brasidus. "Take your hands off me, or I'll have you posted to the most dismal village on all of New Sparta, Sergeant Priam. I am the Archon."

Priam laughed. "So you think you can fool me by saying my name? Every petty crook in the city knows it."

"He *is* the Archon," said Grimes.

"He *is* the Archon," stated Maggie.

"He could just be," said Fenella. "There are techniques of disguise, you know. I've used them myself."

"Call the Palace," Brasidus ordered Aristotle. "The Lady Ellena will identify me."

The showman pressed buttons at the base of the videophone on his desk. Only he could see the little screen but all of them could hear the conversation.

"May I speak to the Lady Ellena, please?"

"Who is that?" demanded an almost masculine female voice, probably that of the duty officer of the Amazon Guard.

"Aristotle, of Aristotle's Arena."

"What business would *you* have with the Lady Ellena?"

"None of yours, woman. I want to speak to her, is all."

"Well, you can't."

"It is my right as a citizen."

"You still can't. She's out."

"She's still at her meeting," said Brasidus.

"What meeting?" demanded the Sergeant.

"Of the Women's Branch of the New Hellas Association."

"You seem to know a lot about her movements," muttered the police officer. He looked as though he were beginning to wonder what sort of mess he had been dragged into. If this scruffy helot were indeed the Archon . . . But surely (so Grimes read his changing expressions) that was not possible. "Get the New Hellas bitches on the phone," he ordered Aristotle. "Get the number of their meeting hall from the read-out."

Aristotle obliged.

Then, "May I talk with the Lady Ellena, please?"

"She is addressing the meeting still," came the reply in a vinegary female voice.

"This is important."

"*Who* are you?"

Before he could answer the Sergeant had pushed his way round to the showman's side of the desk.

"This is Sergeant Priam of the Vice Squad. This is official police business. Bring the Lady Ellena to the telephone at once."

"What for?"

"For the identification of a body."

There was a little scream from the New Hellas lady.

"Bring him round here," ordered the Sergeant, "so that he can look into the video pick-up. And then we shall soon know one way or the other."

Two of the Amazon usherettes obliged.

There was some delay, and then Grimes heard Ellena's voice.

"Is this the body that I'm supposed to identify? But, firstly, he's alive . . ."

"I didn't say a *dead* body, Lady."

"And secondly, I wouldn't know him from a bar of soap."

"It's me," said Brasidus.

"And who's 'me'? I most certainly don't know you, my man, and I most certainly do not wish to know you."

But she did not terminate the conversation.

"Have you any alcohol?" Brasidus asked Aristotle.

"Do you expect me to give you a free drink after all the trouble you have caused?"

"Not for drinking. And, in any case, I will pay you for what I use. Some alcohol, please, and some tissues . . ."

Grudgingly the showman produced a bottle of gin from a drawer and, from another, a box of tissues. He demanded—and received—a sum far in excess of the retail price of these articles. Everybody watched as the Archon applied the gin-soaked tissue to his beard which, after a few applications, returned to its normal color.

"So," said the Lady Ellena, "it is you. I did recognize the voice, of course. But where are you calling from? A police station? And why do you wish me to identify you?"

"I'm at Aristotle's Arena. . . ."

"Oh. Another of your incognito slumming expeditions. And you got yourself into trouble. Really, my dear, you carry the concept of democracy too far. Much too far. For a man of your standing to frequent such a haunt of iniquity . . . I suggest that you order the Sergeant to furnish you with transport back to the Palace. At once."

"You had better not come with me," said Brasidus as Grimes

and Maggie made to follow him and his police escort from the office. "The Lady Ellena regards spacemen as a bad influence. And as for the rest of you . . ." The note of command was strong in his voice. "As for the rest of you, I shall be greatly obliged if no word of tonight's adventure gets out. I am requesting, not ordering—but, even so, I could have your Arena closed, Aristotle, and your performers deported, just as you, Fenella Pruin, could also be deported, after a spell in one of our jails. I am sorry, John and Maggie, that we shall not be able to enjoy the rest of the evening together, but there will be other times. Jason will run you back to the Palace at your convenience.

"A good night to you all."

He was gone, accompanied by the deferential policemen.

"Could we have our pistols back?" asked Paulus.

"Help yourself," said Aristotle.

"Another good story that I am not allowed to use," grumbled Fenella Pruin. "At least, not on this world. But the evening need not be a total disaster." She turned to Grimes. "Perhaps an interview, John? I am staying at the New Sparta Sheraton. . . ."

"And *we*," said Shirl and Darleen, "are staying at the Hippolyte Hotel."

"And I," said Maggie sweetly, "saw him first. Come along, John. We'll find a place for a quiet drink or two before we return to the Palace."

"I'm supposed to be running you back," said Jason sullenly.

"So you are. Come with us, then. But you will sit at a separate table. Don't look so worried. We'll pay for your drinks."

Chapter 9

They had their drinks in an establishment where the almost naked waitresses made it plain that they were willing to oblige in more ways than the serving of drinks and who regarded the few female customers with open hostility. After having had a glass of ouzo spilled in her lap Maggie decided that it was time to leave.

Jason, who had been getting on well with the hostess who had joined him at his table, sharing the large bottle of retsina that had been purchased at Grimes' expense, got to his feet reluctantly. His companion glared at him when he corked the wine bottle and took it with him.

"Waste not, want not, Commodore," he said.

"Too right," agreed Grimes.

"I thought that this wine was a present," complained the overly plump blonde.

"It is," said Jason. "To me."

They made their way to the parked hovercar, got in. The drive back to the palace was uneventful. They entered the building, as they had left it, by a back door. Amazon guards, or guards of any kind, were conspicuous by their absence. Security seemed to be nonexistent. Grimes said as much.

Jason laughed. "If you'd tried to get in this way without me along with you there'd have been a few surprises. Unpleasant ones."

"Such as?" asked Grimes.

"That'd be telling, Commodore. Just take my word for it."

"You're not a native, are you?" asked Grimes, who had detected more than a trace of American accent.

"Nosir. No way. Before I came here I was an operative with Panplanet Security, home office Chicago. Paulus and I brought all the tricks of our trade with us. And now good night to you, Commodore Grimes and Commander Lazenby. I take it that you know the way back to your quarters."

Maggie assured him that they did.

They went to Grimes' suite.

They sat down and talked, discussing the events of the evening, comparing notes.

Maggie asked, "However did you get to know those two New Alice wenches, or, come to that, Fenella Pruin?"

"It's a long, sad story," he said. "At the finish of it I had all three of them as passengers aboard *Little Sister*—the deep space pinnace of which I was owner-master before I bought *Sister Sue*."

"It must have been an interesting voyage."

"Too interesting at times. But there were . . . compensations."

"I'm sure. Knowing you." She sipped from the drink that he had poured her. "It's a pity that we have no power to recruit the Pruin woman. She impresses me as being a really skillful investigator."

"Only when there's a story with sex involved, the only kind of story that *Star Scandal* prints."

"There are other stories, you know, equally interesting, and other media with good money to pay for them. Perhaps if I could get her interested . . . Or if you could. You know her better than I do. Come to that, Shirl and Darleen could do some work for us. . . ."

"Shirl and Darleen? Oh, they'd make quite good bodyguards. They're at their best in a rough and tumble. But as intelligence agents? Hardly."

"As intelligence agents," she said firmly. "Not very high grade ones, but useful. They told you where they were staying."

"The Hippolyte Hotel. But what's that got to do with it?"

"The Hippolyte Hotel is owned by a company made up of members of the New Hellas Association, mainly well-to-do female members. The Lady Ellena is a major shareholder. The name of the place is her choice. As you must have already gathered she has a thing about Amazons. In case you don't already know, Hippolyte was Queen of the Amazons."

"I'm not altogether ignorant of Terran history and mythology."

"All right, all right. But the Hippolyte is much frequented by NHA people. Too, I found out that the Hippolyte offered special rates to the stars now appearing at Aristotle's Arena."

"What's so sinister about that?"

"I . . . don't know. But there have been rumors. All those performers are alleged to be specialists in various offplanet martial arts. As far as your girlfriends Shirl and Darleen are concerned it's more than a mere allegation. Could Ellena be thinking of recruiting instructors in exotic weaponry and techniques for her Amazon Guards?"

"Terrible as an army with boomerangs," misquoted Grimes.

"Very funny. But our own Survey Service Marine Corps Commandos are trained to inflict grievous bodily harm with a wide variety of what many would consider to be archaic weapons."

"Mphm."

"Officially," she said, "you're in charge of this Intelligence Branch operation, whether you like it or not. Not only do you rank me, but you've had more experience in Intelligence work."

"But I didn't have the intelligence to realize it."

"You do now. Anyhow, although I'm officially subordinate to you, I can make suggestions, recommendations. I recommend that you exercise your influence on Shirl and Darleen—they seem to like you, the Odd Gods of the Galaxy alone know why!—and persuade them to accept the Lady Ellena's offer. If she makes it, that is. And if she does, and they do, then perhaps your other girlfriend might stay on here to do a story on their experiences instead of following the rest of the troupe across the Galaxy. . . ."

"This used to be an all-male planet," said Grimes. "But now . . . First you, then Fenella, then Shirl and Darleen. It never rains but it pours."

"You're not complaining, are you?" she asked.

"Certainly not about you," he told her gallantly.

They finished their drinks and extinguished their smokes and went to bed, the bed that Maggie would have to leave to return to her own before the domestic staff was up and about.

Chapter 10

The next morning Grimes was awakened from his second sleep—he had drifted off again after Maggie had left him—by one of the very plain serving maids who brought him a jug of thick, sweet coffee and informed him that breakfast would be served, in the small dining room, in an hour's time. He had some coffee (he would have preferred tea) and then did all the things that he had to do and attired himself in a plain, black shirt and a kilt in the Astronaut's Guild tartan—black, gold and silver—long, black socks and highly polished, gold-buckled, black shoes. He went out into the passageway and rapped on the door to Maggie's suite.

She called, "Who is it?"

"Me."

"Come in, come in."

He was amused to find that she was attired as he was, although her kilt was shorter and lighter than his and the tartan was the green, blue, brown and gold of the Institute of Life Sciences.

"All we need," he said, "is a piper to precede us into the Archon's presence. I wonder if he'll give us haggis for breakfast."

She laughed. "Knowing you, you'll be wishing that he would.

You'll be pining even for Scottish oatmeal. The Lady Ellena's ideas as to what constitutes a meal to start the day do not coincide with yours.''

They most certainly did not. Grimes maintained that God had created pigs and hens only so that eggs and bacon could make a regular appearance on the breakfast tables of civilized people. He regarded the little, sweet buns with barely concealed distaste and did no more than sip at the syrupy, sweet coffee.

The Archon was in a subdued mood. The Lady Ellena looked over the sparsely laden table at her husband's guests with obviously spurious sweetness.

"Do have another roll, Commodore. You do not seem to have much of an appetite this morning. Perhaps your party last night was rather too good."

Grimes took another roll. There was nothing else for him to eat.

"The Archon tells me," she went on, almost as though Brasidus were not among those present, "that you know two of the performers at Aristotle's Arena. Those rather odd girls called Shirl and Darleen. The boomerang throwers."

"Yes," admitted Grimes. "We are old acquaintances."

Maggie was trying hard not to laugh.

"You have no doubt already noticed," went on Ellena, "that I have formed a Corps of Amazons. I considered this to be of great importance on a planet such as this which, until recently, had never known women. Women, I decided, must be shown to be able to compete with men in every field, including the military arts and sciences."

"Mphm," grunted Grimes, pulling his pipe and tobacco pouch out from his sporran.

"Would you mind refraining, Commodore? I am allergic to tobacco smoke. Besides, the ancient Hellenes never indulged in tobacco."

Only because they never had the chance to do so, thought Grimes as he put his pipe and pouch away.

"I am interested," she said, "in recruiting instructors from all over the Galaxy. Brasidus has told me that Shirl and Darleen— what *peculiar* names—are proficient in boxing techniques, especially a sort of foot boxing, and in the use of throwing weapons. Boomerangs."

"The ones that they demonstrated last night," said Grimes, "were only play boomerangs."

"I know, Commodore, I know. After all I, like you, am an Australian. Or, in my own case, *was*. I am now a citizen of New

Sparta. But I have no doubt that the young . . . ladies can use hunting boomerangs, *killing* boomerangs, with effect."

"I've seen them do it," said Grimes.

"You have? You must tell me all about it some time. Meanwhile, I shall be greatly obliged if you will act on my behalf and try to persuade the young ladies to enter my service as instructors."

"Rank and pay?" asked Grimes, always sensitive to such matters.

"I was thinking of making them sergeants," said Ellena.

"No way," said Grimes. "There will have to be much more inducement. As theatrical artistes they are well paid." (Were they?) "They are members of a glamorous profession. I would suggest commissioned rank, lieutenancies at least, with pay to match and specialists' allowances in addition."

"Do you intend to demand a 10 percent agent's commission?" asked Maggie.

He kicked her under the table and she subsided.

Ellena did not appear to have a sense of humor. She said, sourly, "Of course, Commodore, if you wish a recruiting sergeant's bounty, that can be arranged."

He said, "Commander Lazenby was only joking, Lady."

Maggie said, "Was I?"

Ellena looked from one to the other, emitted an exasperated sigh.

"Spacepersons," she said, "consider things funny that we mere planetlubbers do not."

Such as money? thought Grimes.

"Nonetheless," she went on, "I shall be greatly obliged if you will endeavor to persuade Miss Shirl and Miss Darleen to enlist in my Amazon Corps. Need I remind you that you are a shipowner whose vessel makes money trading to and from this world? Perhaps if you could bring yourself to call upon them this very morning. . . ."

"I will come with you, John," said Brasidus, breaking his glum silence.

"But you have forgotten, dear, that there is a Council meeting?"

"I have not, Ellena. But surely such a matter as providing separate toilets for the sexes in the Agora does not demand my presence."

"It does so. The status of women on this world must be elevated and you, as my husband, must make it plain that you think as I do."

"I'd accompany you, John," Maggie told him, "but I'm

scheduled to address the Terra-Sparta Foundation on the history and culture of my own planet. I can't very well wriggle out of it."

"I'll organize transport for you, John," said Brasidus.

"It might be better if I did," said Ellena. "It will look better if the Commodore is driven to the Hippolyte by one of my Amazon Guards rather than by one of your musclebound louts."

So Grimes, in a small two-seater, a hovercar looking even more like an ancient war chariot than the generality of military vehicles on this world, was driven to the Hippolyte Hotel by a hefty, blonde wench who conveyed the impression that she should have been standing up holding reins rather than sitting down grasping a wheel. She brought the vehicle to an abrupt halt outside the main doorway of the hotel, leapt out with a fine display of long, tanned legs and then offered Grimes unneeded assistance out of the car to the pavement. The doorwoman, uniformed in imitation of Ellena's Amazons but squat and flabby (but with real muscles under the flab, thought Grimes) scowled at them.

"What would you, citizens?" she demanded.

"Just get out of the way, citizen, and let us pass."

"But *he* is a man."

"And I am Lieutenant Phryne, of the Lady Ellena's Amazon Guard, here on the Lady's business."

"And *him*?"

"The gentleman is Commodore Grimes, also on the Lady's business."

"All right. All right." She muttered to herself, "This is what comes of letting theatricals in here. Turning the place into a spacemen's brothel."

"What was that?" asked Phryne sharply.

"Nothing, Lieutenant, nothing."

"The next time you say nothing say it where I can't hear it."

Grimes looked around the lobby of the hotel with interest. All its walls were decorated with skillfully executed mosaic murals, every one of which depicted stern-looking ladies doing unkind things to members of the male sex. There was Jael, securing the hapless Sisera to the mattress with a hammer and a nail. There was Boadicea, whose scythed chariot wheels were slicing up the Roman legionnaires. There was Jeanne d'Arc, on horseback and in shining armor, in the act of decapitating an English knight with her long, gleaming sword. There was Prime Minister Golda riding in the open turret of an Israeli tank, leading a fire-spitting

armored column against a rabble of fleeing Arabs. There was
Prime Minister Maggie on the bridge of a battleship whose
broadside was hurling destruction on the Argentine fleet. There
was . . . There was too much, much too much.

Grimes couldn't help laughing.

"What is the joke, Commodore?" asked Lieutenant Phryne
coldly.

"Whoever did these murals," explained Grimes, "might have
been a good artist but he . . ." She glared at him. "But *she*," he
corrected himself, "was a lousy historian."

"I do not think so."

"No?" He pointed with the stem of his pipe at the very
imaginative depiction of the battle off the Falkland Islands. "To
begin with, Mrs. Thatcher wasn't *there*. She ran things from
London. Secondly, by that time battleships had been phased out.
The flagship of the British fleet was an aircraft carrier, the other
vessels destroyers, frigates and submarines. Thirdly, with the
exception of one elderly and unlucky cruiser, the Argentine navy
stayed in port."

"You seem to be very well informed," said the Amazon
lieutenant coldly.

"I should be. My father is an historical novelist."

"Oh."

The pair of them walked to the reception desk.

"Would Miss Shirl and Miss Darleen be in?" asked Grimes.

"I think so, citizen," replied the slight, quite attractive brunette.
"I shall call their suite and ask them to join you in the lobby.
Whom shall I say is calling?"

Before Grimes could answer his escort said, "I am Lieutenant
Phryne of the Lady Ellena's Amazon Guard. This citizen is
Commodore Grimes. The business that we have to discuss is
very private and best dealt with in their own quarters."

The girl said something about hotel regulations.

The lieutenant told her that the Lady Ellena was a major
shareholder.

The girl said that Shirl and Darleen already had a visitor. A
lady, she added.

"Then I shall be outnumbered," said Grimes. "I shall be no
threat to anybody's virtue."

Both the receptionist and the lieutenant glared at him.

Chapter 11

"Come in!" called a female voice as Lieutenant Phryne rapped sharply on the door, which slid open. "Come in! This is Liberty Hall; you can spit on the mat and call the cat a bastard." Then, "Who's your new girlfriend, Grimes? You never waste much time, do you?"

Fenella Pruin, sprawled in an easy chair, her long, elegant legs exposed by her short *chiton*, a glass of gin in her hand, looked up at the commodore. So did Shirl and Darleen, who were sitting quite primly side by side on a sofa, holding cans of beer. Foster's, noted Grimes, an Australian brand, no doubt brought to New Sparta as part of one of *Sister Sue's* cargoes.

"Lieutenant Phryne," said Grimes stiffly, "has been acting as my chauffeuse."

"And what are you acting as, Grimes? What hat are you wearing this bright and happy morning? Owner-master? Pirate commodore? Planetary governor?"

"Recruiting sergeant," said Grimes.

"You intrigue me. But take the weight off your feet. And you, Lieutenant. And find the Commodore a gin, Shirl, and his Amazon Guard whatever she fancies . . ."

After the drinks had been organized Grimes found himself sitting between Shirl and Darleen, facing Fenella.

"Here's to crime," she toasted, raising her refilled glass. "And now, Grimes, talk. What's with this recruiting sergeant business? Let me guess. You're an old boozing pal of the Archon's. The Archon's lady wife is building up her own private army, of which Lieutenant Phryne is a member. Lady Ellena is on the lookout for offplanet martial arts specialists to act as instructors. Right?"

"Right."

"And Shirl and Darleen are not only artists with the boomer-

47

ang but expert in their own peculiar version of *savate*. Boxing with the feet. Right?''

"Right."

"What's in it for them?"

"Lieutenants' commissions. Standard pay for the rank, plus allowances."

"Should we accept, Fenella?" asked Shirl. "It would seem to be a steady job, staying in one place. We are becoming tired of jumping from world to world."

"Leave me to negotiate," said the journalist. Then, to Grimes, "At times I wear more than one hat myself. As well as being a star reporter I am a theatrical agent. Oh, only in respect of Shirl and Darleen. I sort of took them under my wing when you left them stranded on Bronsonia." She added virtuously, "Somebody had to."

"Is it an agent's hat you're wearing?" asked Grimes sardonically. "Or a halo?"

She ignored this and turned to Phryne. "What's lieutenant's pay in the Amazon Corps?"

"One thousand obols a month."

"And what's that in *real* money? Never mind. . . ." She used her wrist companion as a calculator. "Mmm. Not good, but not too bad. And the bennies?"

"Bennies, Lady?"

"Side benefits."

"Free accommodation, with meals in the officers' mess. Two new uniforms a year. A wine ration . . ."

"We do not like wine," said Darleen. "We like beer."

"I think that I could arrange that," Grimes said.

"All the more cargo for your precious ship to bring here," sneered Fenella. "But, anyhow, a generous beer ration must be part of the contract. Imported beer, not the local gnat's piss." Again she turned to Phryne. "What extra pay do instructors get?"

"I cannot say with any certainty. But junior officers often complain that instructor sergeants make more money than they do."

"And a sergeant's pay is?"

"In the neighborhood of six hundred obols a month."

"Which means that they must get at least another five hundred extra in special allowances. Find out how much it is, Grimes, and then argue that a commissioned officer should receive allowances on a much higher scale than a non-commissioned one. And, talking of commissions. . . . What about mine?"

"I do not think," said Grimes, "that the Amazon Corps needs a press officer."

"I wasn't talking about that sort of commission. I was talking about my agent's commission."

"Surely even you wouldn't take money off Shirl and Darleen!"

"I've no intention of doing so, but I expect something for myself for handling their affairs. To begin with, I got some very good coverage of the adventures of the rather tatty troupe that I signed them up with. (Talking of that, I shall expect the Lady Ellena to buy them out of their contract.) Now I shall want coverage of Shirl's and Darleen's experiences in the Amazon Guard. *With The Woman Warriors Of New Sparta* and all the rest of it. Which means that I must be given rights of entry to the Archon's palace at all times . . ."

"I did hear," said Grimes, "that you were given the bum's rush the one time that you came a-calling."

"I was. And I still resent it. Just see to it that it doesn't happen again."

"That is a matter for the Archon."

"Or for the Archoness. But you'll just have to talk her round, Grimes. If she wants Shirl and Darleen, those are the terms."

Grimes looked at her through the wreathing fumes from his pipe. The nostrils of her sharp nose were quivering but he did not think that this was due to the reek of burning tobacco. She was on the scent of something. She could be a valuable ally. Although he and Maggie were attached to the Intelligence Department the muckraking journalist was far more skilled at ferreting out information than they, simple spaceman and relatively unsophisticated scientist, could ever be.

He got to his feet.

He said, "I'll do my best, Fenella."

She said tartly, "There have been times when your best has not been good enough." Then he grinned. "But you usually finish up with what you want."

He turned to Shirl and Darleen. "Thank you for the drinks. And I hope that I'll soon be seeing you in uniform."

Darleen said, rather wistfully, "We would like to be wearing your uniform, aboard your ship."

He laughed and said, "Unfortunately the Merchant Navy, unlike the Survey Service, doesn't run to Marines. . . ."

"Perhaps when you next go a-pirating . . ." said Fenella.

"Mphm," grunted Grimes. (Piracy, to him, was a very dirty word.)

Accompanied by Lieutenant Phryne he made his way out of the suite and then down to the parked hovercar.

Phryne drove back to the palace by a circuitous, sight-seeing route.

She said snobbishly, "Forgive me for speaking my mind, sir, but those . . . ladies are not, in my opinion, even good NCO material. To become a commissioned officer one must possess at least a modicum of breeding."

"And Shirl and Darleen do not?"

"No. You must have seen them. Drinking their beer straight from the can."

"I often do that myself."

"But you're a spaceman, sir. You're different."

"They're from New Alice. They're different."

"You can say that again. And I don't suppose that they'll even know the right knives and forks and spoons to use in the officers' mess."

"I shouldn't worry. That's an art that they've probably picked up since I last knew them. I remember that Miz Pruin tried to bully what she called civilized table manners into them when she and they were passengers on my ship some time ago."

"Miz Pruin . . ." muttered Phryne scornfully. "So now she's to be allowed the run of the Palace. I had the pleasure of being guard commander when she was evicted."

"What have you got against her?"

"She's a muckraker. I've had experience of her muckraking. I'm from Earth originally, as are most of the women on New Sparta, but for a while I was a member of an experimental, all woman colony on New Lesbos. I soon found out that, when it came to the crunch, I was more heterosexual than otherwise but I was stuck there, with quite a few others, until I'd earned enough to pay my passage back home—and a police constable's salary was far from generous. Dear Fenella came sniffing around. She did a feature on New Lesbos for *Star Scandals*. What got my goat was that a photograph of a quite innocent beach party was captioned as a Lesbian orgy. Damn it all, there are nude beaches a-plenty on Earth and other planets!"

"But very few, these days, reserved for the use of one sex only," said Grimes.

"There just wasn't more than one sex on New Lesbos," she said, "just as there wasn't more than one sex here before the planet was thrown open to immigration."

"She's a good reporter," said Grimes.

"The only good reporter is a dead one," said Phryne. "And boomerangs are toys for backward primitives and kicking should be confined to the Association Football field."

Grimes laughed. "I take it, Lieutenant, that you were featured in that famous photograph."

"I was, Commodore. I was wrestling one of the other girls. But men wrestle each other, don't they? And nobody accuses them of being friendly."

Yet another useful word stolen from the English language by an overly noisy minority, thought Grimes.

He said, "What does it matter, anyhow?"

She said, "It matters to me."

Chapter 12

The Lady Ellena received Grimes in her office, listened to what he had to tell her.

She said, "You were overly generous, Commodore—but, of course, it is easy to be generous with somebody else's money. Even so. . . . Commissioned rank for that pair of cheap entertainers. . . ."

He said, "You wanted Shirl and Darleen. Now you've got them."

She said, "I most certainly did not want the Pruin woman. Now it seems that I've got her too."

Grimes told her, "She was part of the package deal, Lady."

Ellena made a major production of shrugging. "Oh, well. At least I shall not have to mingle with her socially. And I think that the Palace will be able to afford to treat her to an occasional meal in the sergeants' mess."

"Or the officers' mess," said Grimes. "Shirl and Darleen will be officers. . . ."

"Thanks to you."

". . . and they will wish, now and again, to entertain their friend."

"I cannot imagine her being a friend to anybody. But now, in *my* palace, she will be free to come and go, to eat food that *I* have paid for, to swill expensive imported beer. But that, of course, is the least of *your* worries, Commodore. After all, it is *your* ship that brings in all such Terran luxuries, at freight rates that ensure for you a very handsome profit."

"Being a shipowner," said Grimes, "is far more worrisome financially than being a planetary ruler. I've been both. I know."

"Indeed?" Her thin eyebrows went up almost to meet her hairline. "Indeed? Well, Your ex-Excellency, I thank you for your efforts on my behalf. And now I imagine that you have business of your own to attend to."

Grimes could not think of any but, bowing stiffly, he made his departure from the Lady Ellena's presence. He was somewhat at a loose end; Maggie was still at her function, giving her after-luncheon talk and answering questions, and Brasidus was still presiding over the council meeting.

He found his way to his quarters. His suite possessed all the amenities usually found in hotel accommodation, including a playmaster. There were gin and a bottle of Angostura bitters in the grog locker, ice cubes in the refrigerator. He mixed himself a drink. He checked the playmaster's library of spools. These included various classical dramas in the original Greek and a complete coverage of the Olympic Games, on Earth, from the late Twentieth Century, Old Style, onwards. Unfortunately the library did not include anything else. Grimes sighed. He switched the playmaster to its TV reception function, sampled the only two channels that were available at this time of day. Both of these presented sporting events. He watched briefly the discus throwing and thought that these people would have much to learn from Shirl and Darleen. Then he switched off and got from his bags some spools of his own. He set up a space battle simulation and soon was engrossed, matching his wits against those of the small but cunningly programmed computer.

Eventually Maggie joined him there.

She flopped into an easy chair, demanded a drink. Grimes made her a Scotch on the rocks. She disposed of it in two gulps.

She said, "I needed that! What a bunch of dim biddies I had to talk to. Oh, it wasn't so much the talking as the stupid questions afterwards. Most of my audience knew only two worlds, Earth and New Sparta, and were quite convinced that those are the only two planets worth knowing. As a real, live Arcadian I was just a freak, to be condescended to. They even lectured me on the glories of Hellenic culture and the great contributions it has made to Galactic civilization. Damn it all, Hellenic culture is only part of Terran culture, just as Australian culture is. . . . Talking of Australians, and pseudo-Australians, how did you get on with Shirl and Darleen?''

"I persuaded them to accept commissions in the Amazon Guard. Unluckily—or was it so unlucky?—Fenella was part of the deal. She's staying on to do a piece on them, and part of the package is that she's to be allowed free access to the Palace at all times.''

"Why did you say, 'or was it so unlucky'?''

"She might be able to help us. I gained the impression that she's on the track of something. Is there any way that she could be pressganged into the Intelligence Branch? After all, we were.''

"But we were—and are—already officers holding commissions in the Survey Service. When admirals say, Jump! we jump. Even you, John, as long as you're on the Reserve List.''

"Civilians can be conscripted . . .'' said Grimes. "*I* was. I became a civilian as soon as I resigned from the Service after the mutiny.''

"As I heard it from Admiral Damien,'' Maggie said, "you were offered the Reserve Commission that you now hold. You were not compelled to accept it.''

"Mphm. Not quite. But there were veiled threats as well as inducements.''

"Could you threaten Fenella?''

"I wish that I could. But as I'm not a major shareholder in *Star Scandals* I can't.''

"Inducements?''

"I've already played one major card by getting her the permission to come calling round to the Palace any time that she feels like it. There should have been a *quid pro quo*. I realize that now.''

"Now that it's too late. What we want is an I'll-scratch-your-back-if-you'll-scratch-mine situation. What inducements can we offer? Mmm. To begin with, I'm the senior officer of the Federation Survey Service on this planet. . . .''

"*I* am,'' said Grimes indignantly.

"But only you and I know it. As far as the locals are concerned, as far as Fenella is concerned, you're no more than an owner-master, waiting here for his little star tramp to come wambling in with her cargo of black olives and retsina. And *I* have a warship at *my* disposal. A minor warship, perhaps, but a warship nonetheless.''

"A Serpent Class courier,'' scoffed Grimes, "armed with a

couple of pea-shooters and a laser cannon that would make quite a fair cigarette lighter. Commanded by a snotty-nosed lieutenant.''

"You were one yourself once. But how far could you trust Fenella? Suppose, just suppose, that you spilled some of the beans to her? Could she be trusted?''

"I think that she subscribes to the journalists' code of honor. Never betray your sources. Too, there's one threat that I could use. The Baroness Michelle d'Estang of Eldorado is a *Star Scandals* major shareholder. I was among those present when Michelle, wielding the power of the purse, killed a really juicy story that Fenella wanted to splash all over the Galaxy.''

"I take it that Michelle is one of your girlfriends.''

"You could call her that.''

"And we've other cards to play. Both of us are personal friends of the Archon. And you, I have gathered, have been on more than friendly terms with Shirl and Darleen. Soon, I think, we must have a get-together with Miz Pruin and offer her our cooperation in return for hers.''

"If you say so,'' said Grimes. "And now I suppose that we'd better get dressed for tonight's state dinner party.''

"We have to get undressed first,'' she said suggestively.

Chapter 13

So there was the state dinner party, as boring as such occasions usually are, with everybody, under the watchful eye of the Lady Ellena, on his or her best behavior, with the serving wenches obviously instructed not to be overly prompt in such matters as the refilling of wine glasses. The female guests, thought Grimes snobbishly, were a scruffy bunch, immigrants all, mainly from Earth, most of whom would never, on their home planets, have been invited to a function such as this. The same could have been said regarding the hostess, Ellena.

What really irked the commodore was the ban on smoking. Not even when things got to the coffee and ouzo stage was he able to enjoy his pipe—and normally he liked to enjoy a couple or three puffs between courses.

He was seated near the head of the high table, with Maggie on his left and the headmistress of the Pallas Athena College for Young Ladies on his right. Maggie had gotten into a conversation with Colonel Heraclion, who was sitting next to her on her other side, leaving Grimes to cope with the academic lady.

"You must already have noticed changes here, Commodore," she said.

Grimes swallowed a mouthful of rather stringy stewed lamb (if it was lamb) and replied briefly, "Yes."

"And changes for the better. Oh, the first settlers did their best to recreate the glory that was Greece but, without the fair sex to aid them in their endeavors, all that they achieved was a pale shadow. . . ."

She waved her fork as she spoke and drops of gravy fell on the front of her chiton. It was rather surprising, thought Grimes, that they succeeded in making a landing as the material of the dress dropped in almost a straight line from neck to lap. He categorized her as a dried-up stick of a woman, not his type at all, with graying hair scraped back from an already overly high forehead, with protuberant pale blue eyes, with thin lips that could not hide buck teeth. Why was it, he wondered, that such people are so often, too often prone to fanatical enthusiasms?

"The founding fathers—there were not, of course, any founding mothers—were spacemen, not Greek scholars," she went on. "They knew something, of course, of the culture which they were trying to emulate, but not enough. It has, therefore, fallen to me, and to others like me, to finish the task that was begun by them."

"Indeed?"

"Yes. For example, you should still be here when the first Marathon is run. It will be a grueling course, from the Palace to the Acropolis. A little way downhill, then on the level and, finally, uphill. The race will be open to *everybody*, tourists as well as citizens."

"Better them than me," said Grimes.

"Come, come, Commodore! Surely you are not serious. Taking part in such an event could be one of the greatest challenges of your career."

"Foot racing," Grimes told her, "is not an activity in which I have ever taken part."

"And I know why," she told him. "You are a smoker. I saw you puffing a pipe outside the banqueting hall before you entered.

But, even so, you could enter. And—who knows?—you might be among those to finish the course. Think of the honor and the glory!''

"Honor and glory don't pay port charges and maintenance and crew salaries," said Grimes.

She laughed. "Spoken like a true cynic, Commodore. A cynic and a shipowner."

"A man can be both," he admitted. "And if one is the latter one tends to become the former."

"A cynic . . ." she trotted out the old chestnut as though it had been newly minted, by herself . . . "is a man who knows the cost of everything and the value of nothing."

"Mphm."

The meal dragged on.

Finally, after the coffee had been served, there was a display of martial arts in the large area of floor around which the tables stood. There were wrestling matches, men versus men, women versus women, men versus women. (The ladies, Grimes assumed correctly, were members of the Lady Ellena's Amazon Guard. He recognized Lieutenant Phryne, although without the leather and brass trappings of her uniform her body looked softer, much more feminine. Nonetheless she floored her opponent, a hairy male giant, with almost contemptuous ease.)

And then it was the turn of Shirl and Darleen. They were already in their Amazon lieutenants' uniforms. (Somebody must have worked fast, thought Grimes.) They had boomerangs, little ones, no more than toys, that, at the finish of their act, seemed to fill the banqueting hall like a flock of whirring birds.

At last it was over, with the boomerangs, one by one, fluttering out through the wide open doorway, followed finally, after the making of their bows to quite enthusiastic applause, by the two New Alicians.

The academic lady was not among those who clapped.

"*Boomerangs* . . ." she muttered. "But they're not Greek . . ."

"I suppose not," said Grimes.

"And those two women . . . If you could call them that. Mutants, possibly. But *officers*. . . . In the elite Amazon Guard. . . ."

"Instructors, actually," Grimes told her.

"Oh. So you know them. You have some most peculiar friends, Commodore. From which planet do they come?"

"New Alice."

"New Alice?" She laughed creakily. "And how did it get its name? Is it some sort of Wonderland?"

"Just one of the Lost Colonies," said Grimes. "Fairly recently rediscovered. A rather odd Australianoid culture."

"Most definitely odd, Commodore, if those two ladies are a representative sample."

"*All* transplanted cultures are odd," he said. "And some cultures are odd before transplantation."

"Indeed?" Coldly.

"Indeed."

The next time Grimes saw a demonstration of boomerang throwing was at the Amazon Guards' drill ground. He stood with Maggie, Lieutenant Phryne and Fenella Pruin. He watched Shirl and Darleen as they hurled their war boomerangs, ugly things, little more than flattened clubs, at a row of man-sized dummies, twelve of them, achieving a full dozen neat decapitations. More dummies were set up. This time Shirl and Darleen improvised, snatching weapons from a pile of scrap metal and plastic, speedily selecting suitably shaped pieces, hurling them with great effect. But there were now no tidy beheadings. There was damage, nonetheless—arms torn off, bellies ripped open, faces crushed.

"Not very effective against well-aimed laser fire," sneered Phryne.

"Better than bare fists," said Grimes. "And, come to that, more effective than your wrestling. . . ."

"Care to try a fall or two, Commodore?" she asked nastily.

"No thank you, Lieutenant."

Maggie laughed and Fenella Pruin sniggered.

And then all three of them watched the Amazons, under the tutelage of Shirl and Darleen, trying to master the art of play boomerang throwing.

"No! No!" Darleen was yelping. "Not *that* way, you stupid bitch. Hold it *up*, not across! Flat side *to* you, not away! And . . . And *flick* your wrist! Like *this!*"

An instructor officer she might be, newly commissioned, but already she was beginning to sound like a drill sergeant.

Grimes, Maggie and Fenella drifted away from the field. They stood in the shade of a large tree. Grimes was amused when Maggie went through routine bug detection; she was taking her secondment to the Intelligence Branch very seriously. There certainly would be bugs in the foliage, he said, but not of the electronic variety. She was not amused.

"Now we can talk," she said.

"What about?" asked Fenella Pruin.

"You."

"Me, Commander Lazenby?"

"Yes. You. You're after a story, aren't you?"

"I'm always after stories. Ask Grimes. He knows."

"And the story with Grimes in it you weren't allowed to publish. *I* know. Do you want to publish the story—if there is one—that you get on New Sparta?"

"Of course."

"Suppose you aren't allowed to?"

Fenella Pruin laughed. "Really, my dear! Even I know that a mere commander in the Survey Service doesn't pile on many Gs."

"A commander," Maggie told her, "with admirals listening to what she has to say."

"Am I supposed to stand at attention and salute?"

"Only if you want to. Anyhow, we can help you, and you can help us."

"*We?* You and Grimes, of all people!"

Maggie contained her temper. "Miz Pruin," she said coldly. "You know why I am here, on New Sparta. Making an ethological survey for the Survey Service's Scientific Branch. You know why Commodore Grimes is here. Waiting for the arrival of his ship so that he may, once again, assume command of her. We know why you are here. Sniffing out a story, the more scandalous the better."

"There's one that I've already sniffed out," said Fenella Pruin nastily. "You're sleeping with Grimes. And if you don't watch him like a hawk he'll be tearing pieces off Shirl and Darleen again."

"He'd better not," said Maggie. "Not while I'm around."

"Don't I get a say in this?" demanded Grimes.

"No matter who is sleeping with whom, or who is going to sleep with whom," went on Maggie, "we, the Commodore and I, could be of help to you. We are *persona grata* in the Palace, as old friends of the Archon. Too, I know my way about this planet. Both of us do."

"You could be right," admitted Fenella grudgingly.

"Of course I'm right. And, on the other hand, although you lack our local knowledge, although you don't have our contacts, you are quite famous for your ability to sniff out scandals. Political as well as sexual."

"Bedfellows often make strange politics," said Fenella.

"Haven't you got it the wrong way around?" asked Maggie.

"No."

It was Grimes' turn to laugh.

Maggie ignored him, went on, "It will be to our mutual benefit if we pool information. The Commodore and I have our contacts. You now have yours—Shirl and Darleen in the Amazon Guard. Too, if you made yourself too unpopular—as you have done on more than one planet—I could be of very real help to you."

"How?"

"You must have seen that Serpent Class courier at the spaceport. *Krait*. Her captain, Lieutenant Gupta, is under my orders. I could see to it that you got offplanet in a hurry should the need arise."

"You tempt me, Commander Lazenby. You tempt me, although I doubt very much that Lieutenant Gupta's flying sardine can is as luxurious as Captain Grimes' *Little Sister*. . . ." She turned to Grimes. "I was really sorry, you know, when I learned that you'd gotten rid of her. We had some good times aboard her . . ."

Grimes could not remember any especially good times, either on the voyage out to New Venusberg or the voyage back. But Maggie, of course, had taken the remark at its face value and was glaring at him.

"Never look a gift horse in the mouth," said Grimes to Fenella, adding, "That's one proverb you can't muck around with."

"Isn't it? Didn't a grazing cow once say, 'Never take a horse gift in the mouth . . .'?"

"Shut up, you two!" snapped Maggie. "Are you with us or aren't you, Miz Pruin?"

"I know what's in it for me," said the journalist. "But what's in it for you?"

"I've told you. Just help in my research project."

"And for Grimes?"

"I'm just helping Commander Lazenby," he said. "Just passing the time until my ship comes in."

"If that's your story," she said, "stick to it. But all right, I'll play. And I'll expect the pair of you to play as well."

"We shall," promised Maggie.

Chapter 14

Fenella Pruin was now allowed into the Palace although she was still far from welcome. Should she chance to meet the Lady Ellena while making her way through the corridors the Archon's wife would sweep by her as though she didn't exist. Brasidus himself would acknowledge her presence, but only just. She was tolerated in the officers' quarters of the Amazon Guard because of her friendship with Shirl and Darleen, both of whom had become quite popular with their messmates. And, of course, she was free to visit Maggie and Grimes any time that she so wished.

She joined them, this day, for morning coffee.

After the surly serving wench had deposited the tray on the table and left, after Maggie had poured the thick, syrupy fluid into the little cups, she demanded, "Well? Have you anything to tell me yet?"

"No," admitted Maggie. "I am still nibbling around the edges, as it were. The New Hellas people are up to *something*. But what?"

"It's a pity that you can't join them," said Fenella.

"It is. But they know that I'm an officer of the Federation Survey Service. And they know that both Commodore Grimes and I are personal friends, old friends of Brasidus." She laughed. "Although if it were not for that personal friendship they might try to recruit John."

"It'd be my ship they'd want," said Grimes. "Not me especially."

"Why not?" asked Fenella. "After all, you were slung out of the Survey Service in disgrace. . . ."

"I resigned," growled Grimes.

"And you were a pirate . . ."

"How many times," he demanded, "do I have to tell people that I was a privateer? And now, Fenella, do you have anything to tell us?"

She looked at him and said, "I was under the impression, Grimes, that the ethological research project was Commander Lazenby's baby, not yours."

"Commodore Grimes," said Maggie, "is helping me with it. Just out of friendship, of course."

"Of course," concurred Fenella, twitching her nose. "Of course. But the Commodore was quite recently a servant of the Federation, on the public payroll, as a planetary governor, no less . . . Are you really self-employed, Grimes? Or is it just a cover?"

"It is a known fact," snapped Maggie, "that Commodore Grimes is an owner-master."

"At the moment," said Grimes, "just an owner. I shall be master again as soon as I get my name back on *Sister Sue*'s register."

"It is the *unknown* facts that interest me . . ." murmured Fenella. "Such as the real reason for the appointment of a notorious pirate . . ."

"*Not* a pirate!" yelled Grimes.

". . . to the governorship of a planet."

"You've trodden on corns in the past," said Grimes coldly. "You should know, by this time, that there are some corns better not trodden on."

Maggie sighed. "All this is getting us nowhere and has nothing at all to do with New Sparta. Would you mind telling us, Fenella, just what you've found out?"

The journalist finished her coffee, said, "No thanks, Maggie. One cup of this mud was ample. Potables shouldn't need knives and forks to deal with them." She took a cigarette from the box on the table, puffed it into ignition. "Now, I think I'm getting places, which is more than can be said for the pair of you. A Major Hera has taken quite a fancy to Shirl and Darleen. She is taking private *savate* lessons and, in return, is teaching the two girls her own version of wrestling. Now, now . . . I know that you have dirty minds, or I know that Grimes has, but there's nothing like what you're thinking. Not yet, anyhow, but I must admit that Shirl and Darleen are surprisingly innocent in some respects. Well, Hera is a high-up in the Ladies' Auxiliary of the New Hellas Association. She's already persuaded quite a few Amazon officers and NCOs to join. She's been trying to persuade the two new Instructor Lieutenants to join. I've advised them to yield to her blandishments and then to keep their eyes skinned and their ears flapping."

"I can't see them as spies," said Grimes. "They're too direct. Too honest."

"Who else have we got?" she asked. "Not me. Not either of you."

"And they will report to you?" asked Grimes.

"Yes," she said.

"They will report to *us*," stated Maggie firmly. "After all, they are Commodore Grimes' friends. What could be more natural than that they should join him here for a drink or two?"

"As long as I am present," said Fenella.

"Talking of drinks," said Grimes, "I could do with a stiff one to wash away the taste of that alleged coffee."

The two ladies thought that this was quite a good idea.

Chapter 15

"You know, John," said Brasidus, "I think that I was much happier in the old days. When I was a simple sergeant in the army, with authority but not much responsibility. Now I have responsibility, as Archon, but my authority seems to have been whittled away." He sighed. "Sparta—it wasn't called *New* Sparta then—was a far simpler world than it is now. We were happy enough eating and drinking and brawling. There were no women to tell us to wash behind the ears and watch our table manners." He gulped from his mug of wine. "I regard you as a friend, John, a good friend, but I have thought that it was a great pity that you ever came to this planet, opening us up to the rest of the Galaxy . . ."

"If it hadn't been me," said Grimes, "it would have been somebody else. The search for Lost Colonies is always going on. I've heard that 90 percent of the interstellar ship disappearances have now been accounted for. And, in any case, how many ships of that remaining 10 percent founded a colony? Possibly none of them."

"You are changing the subject, my friend. In the old days I

should never have been obliged to disguise myself in order to enjoy, with a good friend, what you refer to as a pub crawl. I should never have had to wait for an evening when my wife—my *wife*—was out attending some meeting or other. There weren't any wives.''

"As I recall it," said Grimes, "some of your boyfriends, your surrogate women, could be bitchy enough. And, in any case, the King of Sparta would have done as you are doing now, put on disguise, if he wished to mingle, incognito, with his subjects."

"If he had mingled more," said Brasidus sourly, "he might have kept his crown. And his head. As it was, he just didn't have his finger on the pulse of things."

"And you have?"

"I hope so."

"Tell me, what do you feel?"

"I . . . I wish that I knew."

The two men looked around the tavern, which was far from crowded. They had been able to secure a table at which they could talk with a great degree of privacy. Even the two bodyguards, although not quite out of earshot, were fully occupied chatting up the slovenly, but crudely attractive, girl who had brought them a fresh jug of wine. Had he not already seen how swiftly Jason and Paulus could act when danger threatened Grimes would have doubted their value.

"But you have your Secret Service, or whatever you call it," pursued Grimes. "Surely they keep you informed."

Brasidus laughed. "I sometimes think that the State subsidizes the New Hellas Association and other possibly subversive organizations. They're packed with Intelligence agents, all of them dues-paying members. But do they tell me everything? Do they tell me *anything*?"

"They must tell you something, just to stay on the payroll if for no other reason."

"But do they tell me the truth?" demanded the Archon. "This way, mingling with my people in disguise, I can hear things for myself. There are grumblings—but what government has ever been universally popular? Need I ask *you* that? There are those who want a return to the Good Old Days, a womanless world, and who resent the influx of females from Earth and other planets. There are those who want a society more closely modeled on that of ancient Greece, on Earth, with women kept barefoot and pregnant." He laughed. "There are even those, mainly women, who hanker after some mythical society that was ruled by a woman, Queen Hippolyte, where men were kept in subjection. But that, as you would say, is the lunatic fringe. . . ."

"With the Lady Ellena as a member?" Grimes could not help asking.

Brasidus laughed again. "She is a good wife, I'll not deny that, although perhaps a shade overbearing. And I . . . humor her. She believes, or says that she believes, that the Hippolyte legends are true. Oh, I've tried to reason with her. I've imported books from Earth, Greek histories, and she's condescended to read them. And she says that there has been a conspiracy of male historians to suppress the Hippolyte story, to laugh it away as a mere myth . . ."

"Your scholars had done some ingenious tampering with history and biology before your Lost Colony was found," said Grimes.

"That was different," said Brasidus. "But Ellena . . . I've played along with her, up to a point. I let her form her Amazon Guard. Having toy lady soldiers to play with keeps her happy."

"Toy soldiers?" asked Grimes. "Oh, they probably wouldn't be a match for an equal number of Federation Space Marines, but against ordinary troops they'd give a very good account of themselves."

"You really think that?"

"I do."

There was a brief silence, broken only by the happy squeals of the serving wench who had been looking after Paulus and Jason. Of the serving wenches, rather. The original girl had been joined by another, equally coarsely attractive. The pair of them were sitting on the bodyguards' laps, fondling and being fondled. Grimes filled and lit his pipe, looking toward the door to the street as he did so. He saw the women enter, six of them. A fat blonde, a tall, skinny redhead, four very nondescript brunettes. They were dressed, all of them, in rather tawdry finery, with chaplets of imitation vine leaves intertwined with their tousled hair, latter-day bacchantes—or a sextet of working girls enjoying a night on the tiles. They did not seem to be sober, lurching and staggering as they made their way across the floor, giggling and nudging each other.

"Women," muttered Brasidus, "cannot drink with dignity."

Not only women, thought Grimes, although he was inclined to the opinion that drunken men are somewhat less of a nuisance.

The fat blonde failed successfully to negotiate the quite generous space between Grimes' table and that at which the two bodyguards were sitting. Her heavy, well-padded hip almost

shoved Grimes off his chair. "Gerrout o' my way, you barshtard
. . ." she slurred, glaring at him out of piggy blue eyes that, the
commodore suddenly realized, looked more sober than otherwise.
Two of the other women had gotten themselves entangled with
Brasidus. Wine bottle and glasses were overset.

Simultaneously Jason and Paulus were having their troubles.
Their chairs had gone over backwards and they were sprawled on
the floor, their limbs entangled with those of their female
companions. They were trying to get their pistols out from the
concealed holsters, but without success.

The corpulent innkeeper came bustling up. "Citizens! Citizens!
I must implore you to keep the peace!"

"Keep a piece of this!" snarled the redhead, cracking him
smartly across the brow with a wine bottle.

Grimes tried to get to his feet but two of the brunettes pounced
on him, bore him to the floor. They were surprisingly well-
muscled wenches. Their hard feet thudded into his ribs and
belly. He had enough presence of mind to protect his testicles
with his hands—but that left his head uncovered. A calloused
heel struck him just behind the right ear and, briefly, he lost
consciousness. Then dimly he was aware of the scuffling around
him and the voice of the fat woman—no trace of drunkenness
now—saying sharply, "Now! While he's still out!"

But I'm not still out, thought Grimes, not realizing at first that
she was not talking about him.

He was no longer out but those two useless bodyguards were,
jabbed with needles loaded with some kind of drug by the tavern
wenches. He was no longer out and he raised himself on his
hands and knees, in time to see the six women—no, the eight
women; they had been joined by the two serving girls—hurrying
through the door to the street with Brasidus supported between
them. None of the inn's patrons had made any move to interfere.
Why should they? Drunken brawls were not uncommon.

Somehow he got to his feet. He started toward the door and
then hesitated. Unarmed he was no match for no less than eight
hefty, vicious wenches. He stumbled to where Paulus was
sprawled, face down, on the floor. He fell to his knees, fumbled
in the man's clothing. He found the concealed holster almost at
once, pulled out the pistol. He checked that it was loaded,
cocked the weapon. He had by now recovered sufficiently to
run, albeit painfully, to the door.

To his surprise he did not have to look far to find the kidnappers.
They were standing there, all eight of them, in the middle of the

poorly lighted street, still supporting the unconscious Archon between them.

"Freeze!" yelled Grimes, waving the Minetti.

They turned to look at him but otherwise made no move.

"Release him! At once!"

"If that's the way you want it, buster," said the fat blonde.

The women stepped away from Brasidus. Fantastically his body remained upright. Even more fantastically it seemed to elongate, as though the Archon were becoming taller with every passing second. Grimes stared incredulously. He heard, then, the faint humming of a winch. He looked up and saw, at no great altitude, a dark gray against the black of the night sky, the bulk of a small airship. He started to run forward, to try to grab the feet of his friend. Somebody tripped him. He fell heavily but, luckily for him, retained his grip on the pistol. He sensed that the kidnappers were closing in around him and fired at random, not a full, wasteful burst but spaced shots. Surely, in this scrum, he must get somebody in the legs.

He heard a yelp of pain, then another.

He got to his feet.

Nobody stopped him.

There was nobody there to stop him.

He looked up.

The dirigible was gone, presumably with Brasidus a prisoner in its cabin.

He looked around.

The dirt of the road surface had been scuffed by the struggle. In two places there were dark, glistening stains. Blood. But the women had melted into the shadows, taking their wounded with them. He hoped that the fat bitch was among the casualties.

There was the sound of approaching, running feet. He turned in that direction, holding the pistol ready. He saw who was coming, three policemen, what little light there was reflected from their polished black leather and stainless steel.

Hastily Grimes put the gun into a pocket.

The leading police officer shone his torch full on Grimes' face, although not before the commodore had noticed that he was holding a stungun in his other hand.

He said disgustedly, "*You* again." Grimes thought that he recognized the voice. He went on, "I heard shots. There has obviously been some sort of struggle here. What have you been doing?"

"I haven't been doing anything," said Grimes virtuously if not quite accurately. He tried to fit a name to the owner of the voice. "Sergeant Priam, isn't it? Would you mind not shining that light into my eyes?"

"Certainly, sir. Commodore, sir. And now would you mind telling me what in Zeus's name has been going on?"

"A kidnapping. The Archon. He was snatched by a gang of women, carried away in an airship. No, I didn't get any registration marks or numbers. The thing wasn't carrying lights."

The beam of the sergeant's torch was directed downward.

"And this blood. Whose is it? The Archon's?"

"There was a struggle, as you can see. One or two of the women got hurt."

"You shot them."

"It was better," said Grimes, "than having my head kicked in."

"Let me have the weapon, sir."

Grimes shrugged and passed the weapon over.

He said, "It's not mine. It belongs to one of the Archon's bodyguards."

"And where are they?"

"Inside the inn. Unconscious."

Sergeant Priam sighed heavily. "Why do these things always have to happen to me? You will have to come to the station, sir, to make your report." He laughed. "But you'll find it far easier to make your report to Colonel Xenophon than, eventually, to the Lady Ellena!"

Chapter 16

Grimes told his story. Jason and Paulus, almost recovered, thanks to the administration of the antidote, from the effects of the drug with which they had been injected, told their story. The innkeeper, his head bandaged, told his story. Two witnesses, selected at random from the tavern's customers, told their stories.

Colonel Xenophon, a tall, thin, bald-headed man looking

more like a schoolmaster—but a severe schoolmaster—than a policeman, listened.

He said, "I have known, for some time, of the Archon's nocturnal adventures. I was foolish enough to believe that his professional bodyguards would be capable of protecting him."

"On a normal planet," said Jason hotly, "we should have been."

Xenophon's furry black eyebrows rose like back-arching caterpillars. "Indeed? How do you define normalcy? Is your precious Earth a *normal* planet? Among my reading of late have been recent Terran crime statistics. They have caused me to wonder why any citizen, male or female, is foolhardy enough to venture out after dark in any of the big cities.

"And now, Commodore, you are quite sure that the flying machine which removed the Archon was an airship? Could it not have been one of the inertial drive craft or helicopters that have been introduced from Earth?"

"It could not," said Grimes definitely. "I know an airship when I see one."

"Even in the dark?"

"There was enough light. And the thing was . . . quiet. Just a faint, very faint humming of electric motors."

"So. . . . And in what direction did this mysterious airship fly after the pick-up?"

"I don't know. Those blasted women jumped me. I was fully occupied trying to fight them off."

"Ah, yes. The women. Did you recognize any of them, Commodore?"

"No. But I shall if I run across them again. But, damn it all, Colonel, what are you doing about this crime, this kidnapping? Dirigible airships aren't as common as, say, motorcycles. There can be very few, if any, privately owned. Your Navy has a fleet of lighter-than-air craft. I'd have thought that you'd have started inquiries with the Admiralty, to find out what ships had been flying tonight."

Xenophon smiled coldly. "I should not presume, Commodore, to instruct you in the arts and sciences of spacemanship. Please do not try to tell me how I should do my job. Already inquiries have been made. All the Navy's ships are either in their hangars or swinging at their mooring masts. All Trans-Sparta Airlines' ships, passenger carriers and freight carriers, have been accounted for. And that's all the airships on New Sparta."

"So the ship I saw must either have belonged to the Navy or to Trans-Sparta."

"If you saw such a ship, Commodore. You may have thought that you did. But drugs had been used during the kidnapping. It is possible that during your first struggle with the women an attempt may have been made to put you out by such means and that you may have received a partial dosage, enough to induce hallucinations. Or a blow on the head might have had the same effect."

"If there were no flying machine involved," persisted Grimes, "how was it that the Archon was spirited away from the inn without trace?"

"I think," said the colonel, "that the quarter of the city in which you and the Archon were . . . er . . . conducting your researches is known to Terrans as a rabbit warren. I didn't appreciate the aptness of that expression until I read one of your classics, *Watership Down.* But if you want to lose a needle in a haystack, a rabbit warren is a good place to do it."

"Mphm," grunted Grimes.

"And now, Commodore, may I suggest—may I urge—that you and your two companions return to the Palace; transport will be provided for you. I do not envy your having to tell the story of this night's happenings to the Lady Ellena. She has already been notified, of course, that the Archon is missing. She is a lady of iron self-control but I could tell that she was deeply moved. Please assure her that I and my men will return her husband to her, unharmed, as soon as is humanly possible."

Grimes turned to follow Sergeant Priam from Xenophon's plainly furnished office. The colonel checked him.

"Oh, Commodore, I advise you, strongly, not to try to conduct any sort of rescue operation yourself. Please leave matters in the hands of the experts, such as myself and my people."

"I shouldn't know where to start," said Grimes.

But I shall find out, he thought.

His confrontation with Ellena was bad enough, although not as bad as he had dreaded that it would be.

"Much as I should wish to," she said coldly, "I cannot hold you responsible, Commodore. The Archon was having his 'nights out' . . ." she contrived to apostrophize the phrase . . . "long before you returned to this world.

"Meanwhile, all that I can do is wait. Presumably the kidnappers will present their demands shortly, and then there will be decisions to be made. Until then . . ." She smiled bleakly. "Until then, the show must go on. I shall function as acting Archon until the return of my husband. There will be no disruption of the affairs of state, not even the minor ones such as the Marathon next week.''

She is enjoying this . . . thought Grimes.

He asked, ''What about the Council, Lady?''

She said, ''The Council will do as they are told.''

Or else? he wondered.

She said, ''That will be all, Commodore.''

Grimes considered backing out of the presence but decided not to.

''Who were those women?'' asked Maggie.

''I'll know them if I meet them again,'' said Grimes.

''Could they,'' she went on, ''have been members of the Amazon Guard?''

''No. The Amazon Guard, apart from exceptions such as Shirl and Darleen, goes in for uniformity. Apart from hair coloring all those wenches could be cast from the same mold. The Amazon Guard, I mean. It was a very mixed bunch that we got tangled with last night. The long and the short and the tall.''

''And you're sure about the airship?''

''Of course I'm sure.'' He paused for thought. ''You were snooping around for quite a while before I got here and, as a Survey Service commander, meeting officers in the various New Spartan armed forces. Does the Navy run to any female personnel?''

''No.''

''Trans-Sparta Airlines?''

She said, ''You might have something. Not only do they have women in their ground staff but even token female flight crews. Not in the passenger ships, yet, but in the smaller freight carriers.''

''Do they do any night flying?''

''I don't know, John. You're far more of an expert on such matters than I am. Making an arrival or a departure in a spaceship you always have to check up with Aerospace Control, don't you?''

''And on most worlds there're always some aircraft up and about, at any hour of the day or night. The Aerospace Control computers keep track of them.''

''And suppose certain computer operators wanted to hide the fact that a small airship, a small, freight-carrying airship with a female crew, wasn't where she was supposed to be . . .''

''You've told me *how*,'' he said, ''but not *why*.''

''Or,'' she said, ''*where*? Where have they taken him?''

"I think that he's safe enough," Grimes said. "If they'd wanted to assassinate him they'd have done just that."

"So we start off snooping around Aerospace Control and the Head Office of Trans-Sparta."

"Colonel Xenophon intimated that he'd be taking a dim view if I started making my own investigations."

"But you won't be investigating the Archon's disappearance. As the owner of a ship on a regular run to New Sparta, shortly to be taking command again of that same ship, you're naturally interested in the workings of local Aerospace Control. You can say that you've had a few complaints from your Chief Officer, Mr. Williams, who's been acting Master in your absence."

"Makes sense."

"And I, carrying on with my own research project, will be interested by the part played by women now in the air transport industry. Fenella might care to come along with me to hold my hand."

"A good idea. It's time that she started to pull her weight. Or does she already know quite a lot that she's not passing on to us?"

"It wouldn't surprise me," she said.

Chapter 17

On some worlds the kidnapping of a national or planetary ruler would go almost unnoticed or, at most, evoke only shrugs and muttered comments of "Serve the bastard right!" (There were, of course, those on New Sparta who muttered just that, but careful not to do so in the hearing of those who most certainly would take violent exception to such a comment.) But Brasidus had been popular. He had nursed his world through a transition period, had restored and maintained stability. There were orderly demonstrations outside the Palace, expressions of sympathy and support. There were demands that the criminals—whoever they were—be brought swiftly to justice and the Archon released unharmed.

There was extensive media coverage.

Grimes, Maggie and Fenella studied the story of the kidnapping that was splashed all over the front page of *The New Spartan Times*, together with photographs of Brasidus, Grimes and Colonel Xenophon. "A gang of eight men disguised as women . . ." read Grimes aloud. "Those were no transvestites!" he exclaimed.

"They could have been . . ." murmured Fenella. "There are such people, you know. . . ."

"Those two serving wenches who immobilized Jason and Paulus most certainly weren't transvestites. If they had been, those two so-called bodyguards would soon have found out. Their hands were everywhere. . . ."

"So you admit to being a voyeur," sneered Fenella.

"I couldn't help noticing."

"Then they were accomplices—the serving wenches, I mean—of the six men in disguise."

"Those were not men in disguise!" asserted Grimes. "I should know. I was in violent physical contact with all of them, or most of them, twice. Once inside the tavern, once in the street outside. When you wrestle with somebody, especially somebody dressed in only a flimsy chiton, you soon find out if it's he or she."

"All right," Fenella said. "You're the expert. But it's your word against Xenophon's. What is *he* trying to cover up?"

"And on whose orders?" asked Maggie.

"There could be another explanation," suggested Grimes. "One that makes sense. He's playing cunning, trying to lull the kidnappers into a sense of false security, making them think that he's on a false scent. . . ."

"Or, perhaps," said Maggie, "he doesn't want to antagonize our leading militant feminist, the Lady Ellena, by daring to suggest that members of her sex are guilty of the crime. After all, until Brasidus is released. . . ."

"If he ever is released . . ." said Fenella cheerfully.

"Until Brasidus is released, or rescued," went on Maggie, "Lady Ellena is *de facto* ruler of this world. And—I could be wrong, of course—while she is so, heads are liable to roll."

"Not ours, I hope," said Grimes.

"I don't think so. Not yet, anyhow. I'm Survey Service, and that counts for something. Fenella represents the Galactic Media—and that could count for even more. And you, John, even though she's not quite sure about you, are a wealthy shipowner. . . ."

"Ha!" interjected Grimes scornfully.

". . . with friends in high places."

"With friends like them," said Grimes, "what do I need with enemies?"

"Yes," said Fenella. "You do have friends. As well I know. So . . . There's a cover-up job. So things aren't what they seem. So what are you two doing about it?"

"What are *you* doing about it?" asked Maggie.

"*You* make the news, duckie. I report it."

They told her, then, of their proposed investigations of Aerospace Control and the operations of Trans-Sparta Airlines. Fenella agreed to accompany Maggie, playing the part of an interested journalist, during the visit to the airlines office.

This was not, of course, Grimes' first visit to an Aerospace Control operations center. While he had been in the Survey Service officers, especially those holding command, had been required to gain an inside knowledge of the workings of such establishments. On Botany Bay, after the *Discovery* mutiny, he had been instrumental in setting up Aerospace Control on that planet. Now, as owner-master of a ship on a regular run between Earth and New Sparta, a telephone call was sufficient to secure for him an appointment with the New Spartan Aerospace Control Director.

A sullen, chastened Paulus drove him from the Palace to the spaceport. He did, however, make some attempt at conversation. "That police chief, sir . . . Has he been on to you? He tried to make Jason and me admit that the two girls we were chatting up were . . . *men*."

"You should know," said Grimes nastily. "Were they?"

"What do you take us for?" For a while he concentrated on his driving. "And the worst of it is that he got us to sign a statement that the two little bitches were men. He told us that if we didn't sign it'd be just too bad. For us." There was another silence, then, "One thing we learned on Earth is that it doesn't do to tangle with police chiefs. Not unless you have something on them. And even then. . . ."

There were more police in the streets than usual, Grimes noticed. There was also a police detachment at the airport gates, checking the credentials of all who entered. Paulus had with him an official card of some kind. The police lieutenant sneered when it was produced and said, "Ah, one of the famous bodyguards. I hope that you make a better job of guarding this gentleman's body than you did the Archon's . . ." Grimes produced his passport and other papers; even then it was necessary to make a call from the gate office to Aerospace Control. At last they were let through.

The spaceport control tower was part of Aerospace Control, but only its visible portion. The rest of it, most of it, was underground. Grimes told Paulus to wait in the hovercar. The man didn't like it. He seemed determined to guard *somebody* now that his major charge had been taken from him. But the commodore was firm.

He was expected in the ground floor office. A uniformed—but in spacemanlike black and gold, not pseudo-Greek brass and leather—official, a young woman, escorted him into an elevator which, by its rapid descent to the depths, produced a simulation of free fall. She led him through a maze of brightly lit tunnels, finally into a vast compartment that was all illuminated maps and colored lights, some winking and some steady, in the center of which was a globe depicting Space one hundred thousand kilometers out from New Sparta in all directions. By this was a large desk with its own complement of screens and globes, at which sat the Director.

This gentleman got to his feet as Grimes and his guide approached. The girl saluted smartly and then faded into the background. The Director, a tall, heavily bearded man, like Grimes in civilian clothing, a very plain, gray, one-piece business suit, extended his right hand. Grimes took it.

"Glad to have you aboard, Commodore," he was told. "Of course your ship is no stranger to us here but this is the first time that I have had the pleasure of meeting any of her personnel."

"The pleasure is mine," said Grimes.

"Thank you, Commodore. Will you be seated?" He waved to a chair on the other side of the desk. "You are staying at the Palace, I understand. A most serious business, is it not, this kidnapping of the Archon. What could be the motivation? Money—or politics? Mind you, I should not be at all surprised if those New Hellas people, or whatever they call themselves, are involved." He laughed without humor. "Either they want the Archon to press ahead with what they see as reforms or they want him to put the clock back. I have read their propaganda and I've got the impression that they don't know what they do want."

"Who does?" asked Grimes. Then, "You're not a New Spartan, by birth, are you, Director? I've a tin ear for accents but yours seems to be—let me guess—Rim Worlds. . . ."

"Too right. I was Deputy Director of Aerospace Control on

Lorn and the Director looked like staying put for the next century or so. Then the New Spartan government was advertising for candidates for this job and I applied.'' He grinned. ''I like to think that I run a taut ship.''

''I'm sure that you do, Director.''

''But when you called me, to make this appointment, you sort of hinted that you had some kind of complaint.''

''*I* don't. But, as you may know, although normally I am in command of *Sister Sue* myself I held a ground appointment for a while. . . .''

''A ground appointment!'' chuckled the Director. ''I suppose you could call it that.''

''Yes. During my absence from active command my chief officer, Billy Williams, has been acting master. Captain Williams has been sending voyage reports to me, in my capacity as owner. I have gained the impression from them that he has not been entirely satisfied with New Sparta Aerospace Control's handling of his arrivals and departures.''

''He never complained to me about it. If he has any whinges, Commodore, what are they?''

Grimes affected embarrassment. ''Well, as a matter of fact, Billy—Captain Williams—is inclined to be sexist. When he calls Aerospace Control on any planet he likes it to be a male voice that answers him. All nonsense, of course.'' Grimes looked around the large, dimly lit room. So far as he could see every console, but one, was attended by a male. ''A lot of women would consider you sexist, too. Practically all your staff is male.''

''They wouldn't be,'' said the Director, ''if the Lady Ellena had her way. But even if she did—where would I get trained females from? The girl who brought you in is one of our cadets, but it will be at least two years before she qualifies as a junior controller. And over there, under the airways chart, is Marina. She's a controller third class. She should get her step up and the ones after without any difficulty. She's got a natural feel for the work. . . .''

''Could it be her that my Captain Williams had trouble with? He did say that on his way in he missed a big commercial dirigible by inches. Of course, Billy tends to exaggerate. . . .''

''So it would seem, Commodore. But why don't we stroll over to have a word with Marina?''

The two men walked to where, just over where the girl was sitting, a huge chart of New Sparta, on a Mercatorial projection, adorned the wall. On it little white lights slowly moved, their extrapolated courses fine, luminescent threads. The display, Grimes knew, was computer-controlled and the human operator no more than an observer—but an observer with power to take over should a situation develop with which the electronic brain, lacking intuition and imagination, would be unable to cope.

"Just our normal commercial traffic," said the Director. "The Navy doesn't seem to have any ships up today. They're marked by blue lights. And we don't have any spacecraft coming in or lifting off to complicate the picture." He picked up the long pointer from its rack under the chart, with its tip indicated a spark that, obviously, was making its approach to Port Sparta. "Who is that, Marina?" he asked.

The girl turned in her swivel chair to look up at him. "*City of Athens*, sir," she told him. "She has clearance to come in to her moorings. E.T.A. 1515 hours." Then she saw Grimes standing next to the Director. Her eyes widened but only briefly, very briefly. She was what he would class as a nondescript brunette, smart enough in her uniform, certainly smarter than when he had last seen her, in a dishevelled chiton and those spurious vine leaves entangled in her hair. If it was her, that was. But there was the scent that he had smelled during the struggle in the inn, an animal pungency so pronounced as to be almost unpleasant.

He asked, "Haven't we met before, Marina?"

She said coldly, her manner implying who-the-hell-are-you-anyhow? "I do not think so, sir."

"This is Commodore Grimes, Marina," said the Director. "The owner of *Sister Sue*, and her captain when he's not governing planets."

"I have heard of you, sir," said the girl. Then, "Excuse me. I have to keep an eye on *City of Thrace* and *City of Macedon*; their courses will be close to intersection in an area of poor visibility and turbulence."

She returned her attention to the chart, to the whisper of voices that was coming from the speaker below it.

The Director led Grimes back to his desk.

"Normally," he said, "I'm here only when something interesting is happening. Nothing of interest is happening today and the duty watch is well able to look after the shop. But I thought that you'd like to see how we run things. And it makes a change from my eternal paperwork in my own office."

"How many female controllers do you have?" asked Grimes.

"At the moment, six. One on each watch—that makes three—and the others on non-watchkeeping duties. As a matter of fact Marina isn't on the watchkeeping list; she's filling in for one of the others. Cleo. She had an accident last night. Fell and cut her leg quite badly on a piece of broken glass or something.''

"These things happen," said Grimes.

"And when they happen to people who're overweight they're usually more serious," said the Director.

"These big, fat blondes . . ." murmured Grimes commiseratingly.

"She *is* a blonde," admitted the Director. "But how did you guess?"

"I knew a fat blonde once. And she was always getting into trouble."

The Director laughed and then the two men went up to his private office for drinks and a pleasant enough but inconsequential talk.

Later, in his suite at the Palace, Grimes compared notes with Maggie and Fenella. He told them what he had discovered. "Whoever is behind the kidnapping," he told the women, "has agents, two at least, in Aerospace Control. Traffic officers sufficiently experienced to persuade the average computer to falsify records, to show airships as being where they aren't and not where the screen says they are. One was on duty when I paid my call to the Director. I recognized her. She, of course, recognized me."

"But she didn't know, of course, that you recognized her."

"Well, as a matter of fact she did. After I said, 'Haven't we met before?' ''

"*What!*" The scream from the two female voices was simultaneous. Then, from Maggie, "You bloody fool! They, whoever they are, will know that you're on to them!"

"Not know. Only suspect. All that they will *know* is that I paid a professional call on Aerospace Control and thought that I recognized one of the duty officers. What I am hoping is that their suspicions drive them to do something stupid. . . ."

"And if they do something cunning, where shall we all be?" demanded Fenella. "Oh, you can set yourself up as a decoy— but Maggie and I are in this business too."

"What's done is done," sighed Maggie. "We shall just have to be especially careful from now on."

"And how did your afternoon go?" asked Grimes, changing the subject.

"Successful enough. We just confirmed what we knew already, that Trans-Sparta Airlines have several all-woman flight crews and that these, still, serve only in the freight carriers. We also learned that much of the freight carrying is done by night. Any of five freighters could have been in this vicinity—although, according to the records, not flying directly over the city—at the time of the kidnapping. Of the five, two had female crews. The Trans-Sparta traffic controller was starting to wonder why I, doing social research, was so interested in commercial operations. But I did find out where those two ships were from and, more importantly, where they were bound . . ."

"Unluckily," said Grimes, "it's the deviations and the unscheduled stops that interest us. And those bitches in Aerospace Control will have made sure that there's no record."

Chapter 18

Grimes purchased a large atlas of New Sparta. Among the various maps therein were ones giving details of planetary transport routes—land, sea and air. He studied these, stepped off distances with his dividers. But there was so much territory over which the airships flew, so many stretches where there was not even the smallest village, only a wilderness of forest and mountain. There were so many places at which a dirigible could have made a descent unobserved, even in broad daylight, to disembark willing or unwilling passengers.

Maggie paid more visits to the offices of Trans-Sparta Airlines; her excuse was that she had selected this organization as the subject for her study of the effects of the integration of women into New Spartan industry. Often Fenella would accompany her. She would tell anybody who was interested that she was doing a series which she would call Sex In The Skies, dealing with female air crews on those planets where there were such. She made herself very unpopular by her apparent determination to sniff out evidence of high altitude Lesbian orgies.

Shirl and Darleen continued to function as Instructors in the Amazon Guard. They reported that there was something cooking in the barracks but what they did not know. Despite their popularity with their fellow officers they were still outsiders, not fully accepted.

Colonel Xenophon, whom Grimes met occasionally during the police chief's visits to the Palace to confer with the Lady Ellena, said that promising leads were being followed and that before long the Archon would be released, unharmed, from captivity. He would not say what the leads were. He scorned Grimes' suggestion that some ultra-feminist organization might be responsible for the kidnapping. "I keep on telling you, Commodore," he snapped, "that the gang responsible for the crime was composed of men disguised as women. Furthermore, there is absolutely no record of a dirigible having flown over the city at the time of the kidnap."

Meanwhile, there seemed to be a spate of vanishings, most of those who disappeared having been prominent members of the New Hellas Association. Some bodies were recovered, corpses dumped in back alleys, bearing signs of extreme maltreatment before death. *The New Hellas Courier,* in its editorials, became increasingly critical of both the police force and the administration in general, ranting about the crime wave that had begun with the abduction of the Archon and would not abate until every public-spirited citizen had been disposed of. What, the leader writer demanded, was the Lady Ellena doing about it? But was it coincidence, he continued, that most of those who had vanished or been murdered were opponents of the Lady's feminization programs?

Shortly thereafter the newspaper editor's name was added to the list of Missing Persons.

Meanwhile Ellena governed. Her style was altogether different from that of her husband. Brasidus in his Council had been the first among equals, respected but by no means autocratic. Ellena just gave orders, and if these were not promptly carried out there would be demotions and dismissals. She was not at all displeased, Grimes gathered, by the nickname that had been bestowed upon her. She was not the first Iron Lady in history but certainly was one of the most deserving of that sobriquet.

She did not seem to mind that Grimes and Maggie continued their residence in the Palace, although they were her husband's guests and not hers. She did not object when Fenella continued her visits. She even condescended to mingle socially with the offworlders on occasion, inviting—or commanding—them to official dinner parties. At these the fare was Spartan and the conversation stilted.

And then there was the affair of the bugging.

Just prior to this, Grimes had found indications that his personal possessions, including his papers, had been disturbed during his absences from his suite. He told Maggie, who, after investigation, reported that there were signs that her own things had been interfered with. After this, before every meeting with Fenella, Shirl and Darleen in Grimes' quarters, she would make a sweep with her bug detector, that multi-functional wrist companion which she had been given back on Earth. But the thing, when switched on, did not emit so much as a single *beep*.

This particular morning there was the usual meeting of the five of them with the pretext of coffee and/or other drinks. Before the arrival of the other three, but after the serving wench had brought in the tray, Maggie used the detector, paying special attention to the coffee things. She said, "All clear."

"You like playing with that thing, don't you?" said Grimes.

"I do, rather."

Then Fenella came in, accompanied by Shirl and Darleen.

The two New Alicians were silent while Grimes, Maggie and Fenella compared notes, aired theories, discussed the implications of all that they had learned.

"There's something cooking," said the journalist at last. "I can feel it in my water. Some sort of balloon is about to go up. There is something rotten in the State of Denmark. . . ."

"But this is New Sparta," objected Darleen, "not Denmark. Wherever Denmark is."

"A figure of speech," said Fenella. "And now, let's hear from you two."

"What can we tell you?" asked Shirl. "We are still trying to teach those thick-witted Amazons how to throw a boomerang. And there are the foot-boxing lessons. They are rather better at that."

"What about the private lessons you are giving to that butch blonde, Major whatever-her-name-is?" Fenella's nostrils were quivering, a sure sign that she was on the scent of some interesting dirt. "Has she been giving *you* any lessons?"

"What could she give us lessons in?" asked Darleen innocently. "But she wants to be our friend; she has told us as much. And when we are alone with her we are to call her by her name, Hera, and not address her by her rank."

"All girls together," sneered Fenella. "And haven't you learned yet that the word 'friend' has, over the past few years, acquired a new meaning?"

"We do not understand," said both girls as one.

"But haven't your relations with the major," persisted Fenella, ''been rather warmer than one would expect between a relatively senior officer and two very junior ones?''

''We would not know,'' said Shirl. ''This is the first time that we have been part of an army.''

''Perhaps Hera has been generous,'' said Darleen doubtfully. ''She gives us presents. Like this. . . .''

She raised her right arm. Around the wrist was a broad bracelet of gold mesh, set with sparkling, semi-precious stones.

''It is very pretty . . .'' said Maggie.

''She'll be wanting something for that . . .'' said Fenella.

''Use your detector, Maggie!'' snapped Grimes.

''But . . .''

''Do as I say!''

Maggie pressed the right buttons on her wrist companion. The *beeps* that it emitted seemed deafeningly loud.

''How . . . How did you guess?'' asked Fenella.

''My mind isn't as suspicious in the same way as yours,'' Grimes told her, ''but it has its moments. And isn't there an old saying, beware the Greeks when they come bearing gifts?''

He was rather annoyed when he had to explain the allusion to Shirl and Darleen. And Darleen was even more annoyed when Maggie made her take off the bracelet and then hammered it with the heel of her sandal until her bug detector made it plain that it had ceased to function.

And Grimes realized that they all had behaved foolishly, even to the officer who had fitted Maggie out for her role as intelligence agent. That bug detector should have given a visual warning, not a series of loud beeps. And, beeps or no beeps, the counter-intelligence listeners-in should never have been told that their bug had been detected; instead they should have been fed false information.

But it was no use crying over spilt milk.

Chapter 19

The next day they made a break in what had become their routine.

Instead of the morning meeting in Grimes' suite they did their talking during a stroll through the city streets. This was no hardship; the day was fine, pleasantly warm. But there were problems. A group of five people find it hard to hold a conversation while walking, especially if what is being discussed is of a confidential nature. Raised voices attract attention. So it was that Shirl and Darleen, who did not have much to contribute in any case, brought up the rear while Grimes walked between Maggie and Fenella.

There seemed to be an air of expectancy in the streets. Grimes remarked on this.

"It's the Marathon, of course," said Fenella. "Even though Brasidus is not here to fire the starting pistol, the show must go on."

"It can go on without me," laughed Grimes.

"Some gentle jogging would do you good," Maggie told him.

"There are better ways of taking exercise," he said.

He turned into a shop doorway, where he would be sheltered from the light breeze, to fill and to light his pipe. An annoying eddy blew out the old-fashioned match that he was using. He bent his head to shield the flame of the second match. Something whistled past his ear. He stared at the tiny, glittering thing that had embedded itself in the wooden door frame with a barely audible *thunk*. He recognized it for what it was. He had fired similar missiles himself while taking part in a *panjaril* hunt on Clothis, a combination of sport and commercial enterprise, the beasts being not killed but merely rendered unconscious, then to be shorn of their silky fur and left to recover to wander off and grow a new coat. It was an anesthetic dart that had just missed him.

He forgot the business of pipe lighting, stared at the passing pedestrians, alert for the sight of a gleaming weapon, an aiming hand.

"What's wrong?" asked Maggie.

He indicated the dart, said, "Somebody's out to get us."

"But who?" demanded Fenella.

"You tell me."

"It must be somebody," said Maggie, making a sweeping gesture with her hand at the passersby.

She was as lucky as Grimes had been. The dart that should have struck the exposed skin of her wrist embedded itself harmlessly in the baggy sleeve of her shirt, just above the elbow. Grimes pulled the thing out before it could do any damage, dropped it into a convenient grating in the gutter.

"Let's get out of here!" he snapped. "Back to the Palace!"

"There's never a policeman around when you need one," complained Fenella. Then, "But whose side are they on, anyhow?"

The general flow of foot traffic was now in the direction that they wanted to go. There were very few vehicles. They mingled with the crowd which, although it afforded some protection, hampered their progress. A fat man, past whom Grimes shoved none too gently, uttered a little squeal and collapsed. Grimes saw the tiny dart protruding from his bulging neck. Other people in the immediate vicinity of the fugitives were falling. The members of the hit squad were showing more determination than accurate marksmanship but, sooner or later, they must hit at least one of their designated targets. And how many of the ambulance attendants, out in force as always during a major sporting event, were the genuine article? Would Grimes or his companions be taken to a first-aid station or hospital or to some interrogation center?

Their scattering throughout the crowd was not altogether intentional but it made the pursuers' task more difficult. Had they stayed in a tightly knit group it would have been easy to identify them, to pick them off one by one. As it was, the only two easily indentifiable were Shirl and Darleen, and they were not the prime objectives.

They pushed and jostled their way along the narrow, winding street. They came to the intersection with the main road—not much wider, little more direct—to the Palace. There the crowds were heavy, lining each side of the thoroughfare. There were shouts and cheers. *For us?* wondered Grimes dazedly. He was aware that Maggie had found her way to his side and that Fenella was elbowing her way toward them both through the crush. And there were Shirl and Darleen. Darleen plucked a dart from one of the leather cross-straps of her uniform, dropped it to the ground. The unfortunate, barefooted woman who trod on it also dropped.

And they were pounding down the hill from the Palace, thousands of them, citizens and tourists, men and women, running, as was the ancient Greek custom, naked. It would be impossible to make any headway, toward refuge, against that mob. The first runners were abreast of them now—a slim young woman, her long legs pumping vigorously, her breasts jouncing; a wiry, middle-aged man; a fat lady, her entire body a-quiver who, on the down-grade, gravity-assisted, was putting on a fair turn of speed. It was probably against the rules but it was happening nonetheless; onlookers were casting aside their clothing and joining the runners.

One did so from near to where Grimes and Maggie were standing. He thought that he recognized the back view of her, that mole, with which he had become familiar, on her left shoulder. . . . But . . . Fenella?

"Quick!" snapped Maggie. "Get your gear off. Join the mob!"

Yes, it made sense. Clothed, among the naked runners, they would be obvious targets. Naked they would be no more than unidentifiable trees in a vast forest. But . . .

"My pipe . . ." he muttered. "My money . . . My credit cards . . ."

"Carry your notecase in your hand if you have to. As for your stinking pipe, you know what you can do with it. You've more than one, haven't you? Hurry up!"

He threw off his shirt, unbuckled the waistband of his kilt, remembering just in time to remove his notecase from the sporran. In the crush he had trouble with his underwear, his shoes and his long socks. Then he was stripped, as Maggie was, and the pair of them were out onto the road, merging with the mainstream of runners. Shirl and Darleen were just ahead of them; even with their peculiar hopping gait their nudity made them almost undistinguishable from the crowd.

Grimes ran. He knew that if he dropped back among the stragglers he would once again become a target. Not many men on New Sparta had outstanding ears. The same would apply if he achieved a place among the leaders—but there was little chance of that. He ran, trying to adjust the rhythm of his open-mouthed breathing to that of his laboring legs. He kept his eyes fixed on the bobbing buttocks of the lady ahead of him; there could have been worse things to watch. The soles of his feet were beginning to hurt; except on sand or grass he was used to going shod.

He ran, clutching his wallet in his right hand, using his left, now and again, to sweep away the sweat that was running down his forehead into his eyebrows, then into his smarting eyes.

He snatched a glance to his left. Maggie was still with him, making better weather of it than he was although her body was gleaming with perspiration and her auburn hair had become unbound. She flashed a smile at him, a smile that turned into a grimace as she trod on something hard. She was developing the beginnings of a limp.

But they were keeping up well, the pair of them, although the crowd around them was thinning. Fenella was still in front; Grimes caught a glimpse of a slim figure with a distinctive mole on the left shoulder when, momentarily, he looked up and away from the shapely bottom that he had been using as a steering mark. Shirl and Darleen were nowhere to be seen.

Somebody was coming up on him from astern. He could hear the heavy breathing, audible even above the noise of his own. He wondered vaguely who it was. Then he heard the sound of a brief scuffle and the thud of someone falling heavily and, almost immediately, the shrill whistle of one of the Marathon marshals summoning a first-aid party.

From his right Shirl (or was it Darleen) said, "We got her."

Grimes turned his head. The New Alician was bounding along easily, showing no effects of physical exertion.

"Got . . . who?" he gasped.

"We did not find out her name. A tall, skinny girl with red hair. She had one of those little needles in her hand. She was going to stick it in you. We stuck it in her."

"Uh . . . thanks . . ."

"We are watching for others."

She dropped behind again.

Grimes ran. His feet hurt. His legs were aching. His breath rasped in and out painfully. Maggie ran. Obviously the pace was telling on her too. Fenella ran, falling back slowly from her leading position. The woman ahead of Grimes gave up, veering off to the side of the road. In his bemused condition Grimes began to follow her but either Shirl or Darleen (he was in no condition to try to work out which was which) came up on his right and nudged him back on the right course.

Other people were dropping out. That final, uphill run was a killer. Grimes would have dropped out but, as long as Maggie and Fenella kept going he was determined to do the same. His vision was blurred. The pounding of his heart was loud in his ears. He was aware of a most horrendous thirst. Surely, he thought, there would be cold drinks at the finishing line.

He raised his head, saw dimly a vision of white pillars, of gaily colored, fluttering bunting. He forced himself to keep going although he had slowed to little better than a tired walk. "We're almost there . . ." he heard Maggie whisper and, "So bloody what?" he heard Fenella snarl.

There was a broad white line painted across the road surface.

Grimes crossed it, then sat down with what he hoped was dignified deliberation. Beside him Maggie did likewise, making a better job of it than Grimes. Fenella unashamedly flopped. Shirl and Darleen stood beside them.

An attendant brought mugs of some cold, refreshing, faintly tart drink. Grimes forced himself to sip rather than to gulp.

The Lady Ellena said, "So you ran after all, Commodore . . ."

Grimes looked up at the tall, white-robed woman with the wreath of golden laurel leaves in her hair.

"Unfortunately," she went on, "I shall not be able to award you a medallion for finishing the course. You were not an official entrant and, furthermore, did not begin at the starting point. That applies to all of you."

"Still," said Grimes, "we finished."

"Yes. You did that." She turned to Shirl and Darleen. "What happened to your uniforms, Lieutenants? You realize, of course, that the cost of replacement will be deducted from your pay."

She strode away among a respectful throng of officials.

Other officials conducted Grimes and the others to a tent where they were given robes and sandals, and more to drink, and told that transport would be provided for them, at a charge, to take them to where they wished to go.

It was just as well, thought Grimes, that he had clung to his money and his credit cards all through the race. The Lady Ellena did not seem to be in a very obliging mood.

Chapter 20

Grimes and his companions missed the beginning of the riot.

They had intended to return to the Acropolis after much needed showers and a resumption of clothing to witness the handing out of the awards to the Marathon winner and to those who had placed second and third, but there was too much to be discussed and, too, none of them, with the exception of Shirl and Darleen, felt like making the effort.

Their hired hovercar stopped briefly at the Hippolyte, where Fenella picked up from her room a bag with clothing and toilet articles, then continued to the Palace. Shirl and Darleen went to their quarters to clean up and to put on fresh uniforms, Fenella was given the freedom of Maggie's bathroom, Grimes and Maggie shared a shower in his. Finally all of them gathered in Grimes's sitting room.

They sprawled in their chairs, sipping their long, cold drinks. Grimes was making a slow recovery. The muscles of his legs were still aching but the pain was diminishing. His feet still hurt, but not as much as they had been. His pipe, an almost new one, would soon be broken in, although it was not yet as good as the one that he had abandoned with his clothing prior to taking part in the race.

"Who were they?" asked Maggie. "Why were they gunning for us?"

"The same bitches who kidnapped your cobber, the Archon," said Fenella. "And it was Grimes who put them wise to the fact that we were on their trail when he said that he recognized that wench in Aerospace Control."

"I've lured them out into the open," said Grimes.

"So you say," sneered Fenella. "The way things are, they'll soon be driving us into hiding or, even, offplanet. It's just as well, Maggie, that you have that courier of yours, *Krait*, standing by."

87

"I still think," said Grimes stubbornly, "that they'll over-reach themselves and do something stupid."

"I'm beginning to think," said Fenella, "that that's your monopoly."

"We might as well see what we're missing," said Maggie.

She got up from her chair with something of an effort, switched on the big playmaster, set the controls for TriVi reception. The screen came alive with a picture of the floodlit Acropolis and from the speakers issued the sound of rattling, throbbing drums and squealing pipes. The camera zoomed in to the wide platform upon which Ellena, white-robed, gold-crowned, sat in state, with behind her rank upon rank of her Amazon Guards in their gleaming accoutrements.

"They said that we could not be there," complained Shirl.

"They say that our bodies are not . . . uniform," explained Darleen.

Yes, thought Grimes, looking into the screen, the Guards on display had been carefully selected for uniformity of appearance. They could have been clones.

The camera panned over the crowd. A broad path, lined on each side with police, had been cleared through it. Along it marched a band of women—Amazon Guards again—some with trumpets, some with pipes, some with drums. There were cheers and—surprisingly—catcalls. "Pussies go home! Pussies go home!" somebody was yelling. Other men took up the cry.

The voice of the commentator overrode the other sounds.

"And now, citizens, here, marching behind the band, come the winners to receive their awards from the Lady Ellena. First, Lieutenant Phryne, of the Amazon Guards. . . ." Phryne was not in uniform but in a simple white chiton, with one shoulder bare, with her long, muscular legs exposed to mid-thigh, her golden hair unbound. "And behind her, citizens, is First Officer Cassandra, of Trans-Sparta Airlines, a real flyer. . . ." Cassandra, a brunette, was dressed as was Phryne. "And in third place, Sergeant Hebe, of the Amazon Guards. . . ."

More cheers—and more boos.

"The race was fixed!" somebody shouted, not far from one of the microphones. A struggle was developing, with men trying to break through the police cordon. The band marched on and played on, missing neither a step nor a note. The three Marathon winners marched on, heads held high and disdainfully. Behind them came more Amazons—and the spears that they carried looked as though they were for use as well as for ornament.

Reaching the platform the band split into two sections, one to either side of the steps leading up to it. Ellena rose to her feet. There were cheers and boos, and men shouting. "We want Brasidus! We want Brasidus!" and, "Send the bitch back to where she came from!"

An Amazon officer handed Ellena a golden laurel wreath, its leaves not as broad as the one that she was wearing but broad enough. Phryne bowed, then fell to one knee. Ellena placed the wreath on her head. Phryne got gracefully to her feet and was embraced by the Archoness.

The camera lingered only briefly on this touching scene then swept over the crowd. Scuffles were breaking out all over. A group of four women had a man down on the ground and were kicking him viciously. Elsewhere there was the wan flicker of energy weapons where police were using their stunguns. A woman, her clothing torn from her, was struggling with half a dozen men whose intention was all too obvious. At the foot of the platform the bandswomen had dropped their instruments and had drawn pistols from their belts—not the relatively humane stunguns but projectile weapons—and the escorting guard were already using their spears to fight off attackers, employing the butts rather than the points, but how long would it be before they reversed them?

"Hell!" swore Fenella, "I should have been there, not watching it on TriVi. . . ."

"Be thankful that you're not," Grimes told her. "Women seem to be in the minority in that mob. Speaking for myself, a sex riot is something I'd rather not be involved in. . . ."

Ellena was standing there on the platform, her arms upraised, shouting something. What it was could not be heard. There were the shouts and the screams and, at last, the rattle of automatic fire. Somebody was using projectile weapons. The bandswomen, machine pistols jerking in their hands, were joining their spear-wielding sisters in the defense of the front of the platform. And the spears had been reversed and the blades of them were glistening red in the harsh glare of the floodlights. And whose side were the police on now? Twenty of them, in their black leather uniforms, were charging the Amazons. The weapons in their hands were only stunguns but, to judge from the visible discharge, more of a flare than a flicker, and from the harsh crackle that was audible even in the general uproar, their setting was lethal rather than incapacitating.

The arrival of the first of the inertial drive transports was, at first, almost unnoticed, the clatter of its propulsion unit just part of the general cacophony. It dropped into camera view, and dropped, until it was over the platform, just clear of the heads of those standing there. Pigsnouted in respirators, Amazons dropped from its belly, bringing with them more respirators for their sisters already engaged in the fighting. A high ranking officer, to judge by the amount of brass on her leather, conferred with Ellena, obviously persuading her to mount the short ladder that had now been lowered from the aircraft. The Archoness, followed by the Amazon colonel, embarked.

The TriVi commentator was valiantly trying to make himself heard. "Citizens! I beseech you all to stay away from the Acropolis! This is not just a riot; this is a revolution! People have been killed! They. . . ." His voice faded, recovered. "They are using gas. . . ."

They were using gas. It was what Grimes himself would have done in the circumstances, what he had done, on more than one occasion, during his Survey Service career. From the low-flying aircraft a dense mist, opalescent in the flood lighting, was drifting downward and battling men and women were dropping to the ground unconscious, police and civilians, all except the Amazon Guards in their protective masks. People on the outskirts of the mob, not yet affected, were beginning to run, away from the Acropolis, while others were binding strips torn from their clothing about their faces, delaying the effect of the anesthetic vapor by only seconds.

Hand weapons were being fired at the transport but ineffectually, and the marksmen got off only a few rounds before falling to the ground unconscious. There was even one man who was tearing up cobblestones and hurling them skyward. Darleen remarked scornfully, "He could not hit the side of a barn even if he was inside it."

But he, whoever he was, was at least trying, thought Grimes. He was fighting back.

Another voice came from the speakers, a female one, distorted and muffled as though by breathing apparatus.

"Citizens! You have seen what has been happening at the Acropolis. Certain elements have tried to attack the person of our beloved leader, the Lady Ellena. The assassination attempt has been foiled. The instigators will be brought to justice. And now, all of you who have been watching this on the screens in your homes. . . . Stay in your homes. Do not take to the streets. Security patrols are abroad, with orders to take strict measures to maintain the peace . . ."

"In other words," muttered Grimes, "shoot first and ask questions afterwards."

The last picture on the screen, before the transmitter was shut down, was a dismal one. It had started to rain. Moving among the sprawled, unconscious bodies were gasmasked Amazons. They seemed to know whom they were looking for, were picking up selected prisoners and throwing them roughly into the rear of a large hovercar. Those who were left on the ground were the lucky ones. They would awake in a few hours time cold and wet and miserable—but they would not be awakening in jail.

"And what was all that about?" asked Fenella at last.

"That," said Maggie, "is for us to find out."

Then there was a great hammering on the door.

"Open up!" yelled a female voice. "In the name of the Lady Ellena, open up!"

Chapter 21

First into the sitting room were two Amazon privates, stunguns in hand. They were followed by a major, and behind her was Ellena herself, still in her white robes, still with the golden laurel wreath crown.

"What are you two doing here?" snapped the officer.

"But, Hera . . ." began Shirl.

"The correct form of address, Lieutenant, is 'Madam.' Please remember that."

"This is our free time, Madam," said Darleen rebelliously.

"Free time, Lieutenant, is a privilege and not a right. And don't you know that during this emergency all leave has been suspended? Get back to your quarters. At once."

"Better do as the lady says," advised Fenella.

"Quiet, you!" snarled Hera.

Fenella subsided. Grimes didn't blame her. He would not have liked to try conclusions with that female weight-lifter, her muscles bulging through the leather straps of her uniform. Shirl and Darleen got to their feet, cast apologetic glances at Grimes. He managed a small smile in return. They slouched out of his sitting room in a most unofficerlike manner.

"And what are *you* doing here?" demanded Ellena, addressing the journalist.

"Enjoying a quiet drink with my friends, Lady," she replied defiantly.

"Cooking up some scurrilous stories for the scandal sheets that employ you as their muckraker, you mean," said Ellena. "However, since you are here you may stay. In fact, you will stay. For your own protection. I can not guarantee the safety of any offworlders at large in the city at this time."

"You mean," said Fenella, "that you want to be able to keep an eye on me."

"Somebody has to," Ellena told her. She turned to Maggie. "You, Commander Lazenby, are the senior Federation Survey Service officer at present on this planet. My understanding is that I, as ruler of a federated world, have the right to demand the support of the Federation's armed forces during times of emergency."

Maggie looked questioningly at Grimes, who nodded.

Ellena sneered. "Of course the Commodore, the ex-planetary Governor, is an expert on such matters, especially since the Federation's armed forces on Liberia were doing their damnedest to depose him. But what do you say, Commodore Grimes?"

"You are right in your understanding, Lady," admitted Grimes.

"Thank you, thank you. And now, Commander Lazenby, am I to understand that Lieutenant Gupta, captain of the courier *Krait,* is technically under your orders?"

"Yes."

"And how is this *Krait* armed?"

Once again Maggie looked questioningly at Grimes.

He said, "I was once in command of such a ship myself, Lady. A Serpent Class Courier is no battle cruiser. There will be a forty-millimeter machine cannon, a laser cannon, a missile launcher and a *very* limited supply of ammunition. In a small vessel the magazines are also small, so the laser cannon will be the only weapon capable of sustained firing."

"And are there—what do you call them?—pinnaces?"

"Nothing so big. Just a couple of general purpose spaceboats. Inertial drive, of course. Each can mount a light machine gun if required."

"Still," she said, "a useful adjunct to my own defense forces."

"What about your Navy?" he asked.

She said, "I shall be frank, Commodore Grimes. You know

what this world was like when it was an all-male planet. Many senior officers, in the Army and the Navy, pine for those so-called Good Old Days and too many junior ones believe the rubbish that their seniors tell them. They resent having to take orders from a woman. I cannot trust them.''

"When we get Brasidus back," said Fenella spitefully, "he'll bring them back into line.''

"Until such time," Ellena said coldly, "I must rule as best I can.''

She did not, thought Grimes, seem to be overly worried about the safety of her husband. She was not, even, overly worried about her own safety. There was an arrogance, but not a stupid arrogance. She would take whatever tools came to hand to build up her own position. She had already forged such a tool, her Corps of Amazon Guards. And the Amazons had been brought into being well before the abduction of the Archon.

The telephone buzzed.

Grimes got up from his chair to answer the call. His way was blocked by Major Hera. It was Ellena who took her seat at the desk on which the instrument was mounted.

"Archoness here," she stated.

"Lady, this is Captain Lalia, duty commander of the Palace Guard. There is a mob approaching, with armored hovercars in the lead. If you will switch on your playmaster to Palace Cover you will have pictures.''

"Thank you, Lalia. Commodore Grimes, will you get us coverage as Lalia suggests? Major Hera, if the Colonel is not back yet from the city will you take charge of the defense? I shall remain here for the time being.''

Hera hurried out, leaving the two Amazon privates to guard Ellena. Grimes fiddled with the controls of the playmaster. The picture, being taken by the infrared cameras on the palace roof, was clear enough. It was more of an army than a mere mob that was pouring up the road. There were the armored hovercars in the lead, with their heavy automatic weapons and their uniformed crews and the pennants streaming from their whip aerials. There were motorcycles, and their riders were police, in their stainless steel and black leather uniforms. There were marching civilians, more than a few of whom were carrying firearms.

Directional microphones were picking up the shouts.

"Scrag the bitches! Scrag the bitches! Ellena out! Ellena out!''

"Somebody out there," remarked Fenella, "doesn't like you.''

Surprisingly Ellena laughed. She said, "They will like me

even less in a minute or so. My Amazons will be more than a match for this rabble."

"There're Army personnel there," said Grimes. "And Police."

"I do not need to be instructed, Commodore, regarding the uniforms worn by my own armed forces."

"They aren't behaving as though they belong to you," said Fenella.

"Guards," snapped Ellena, "if that woman opens her mouth again, gag her!"

The mob—or the army—was closer now. Was that Colonel Heraclion in one of the leading armored cars? Yes, Grimes decided, it was, making his identification just before the colonel pulled on a respirator. Gas had been used to quell the riot at the Acropolis; if it were used here it would not be so effective. Police and Army personnel, at least, would have their protection.

The camera shifted its viewpoint, covering, from above, the main entrance to the Palace. Something was rolling out, a huge, broad-rimmed wheel, almost a short-axised cylinder. Gathering speed, it trundled down the road toward the attackers. It was followed by another, and another. Laser fire flickered from the hovercars and there were muzzle flashes and streams of tracer from the heavy machine guns. There were the beginnings of panic, with vehicles attempting to pull off the road, their way blocked by the heavy, ornamental shrubbery. But these were only relatively light armored cars, not heavy tanks.

The first of the wheels—it must have been radio-controlled—exploded. The second one leaped the crater before being detonated. The third one did not have much effect—but this was because the majority of the marchers had been able to run clear to each side, off the road.

"A very old weapon," said Ellena smugly, "but improved upon."

Grimes stared at the picture in the screen, at the shattered vehicles, some of which were still smoldering, and at the contorted, dismembered bodies, some very few of which were still feebly twisting and jerking.

He said bitterly, "I hope you're satisfied."

She said, "They're only men. Besides, they asked for it and they got it."

"Didn't you rather overreact?" asked Grimes.

"Come, come, Commodore. Speaking for myself, I would rather overreact to a threat than be torn limb from limb." She got up to leave. "I do not care what sleeping arrangements you make but all three of you are confined to the Palace, to the two suites allocated to Commander Lazenby and Commodore Grimes.

"A very good night to you all."

She swept out, followed by the two Amazon privates.

"The manipulating bitch!" exclaimed Fenella, not without admiration. "You know, I almost hope that she pulls it off."

"If she does," said Grimes, "this is one world that I shall do my best to avoid in the foreseeable future."

Chapter 22

So they were, to all intents and purposes, prisoners in the Palace.

It was decided that Fenella would take up residence in what had been Maggie's suite and that Maggie would move in with Grimes. Everybody must already know that she had been sleeping with him; now it would be made official. Maggie said that she would call Lieutenant Gupta to let him know that his services might be required but was unable to get through to the spaceport. She tried direct punching first but without results. Then she got through to the Palace switchboard. A young lady in Amazon uniform politely but coldly informed her that during the state of emergency no outward calls were allowed.

After this the three of them watched the playmaster to try to catch up with the news. There was a speech by Ellena, which she delivered from before a backdrop on which were idealized portraits of such famous persons as Prime Ministers Indira Gandhi, Golda Mier and Margaret Thatcher. There was also one of a lady attired as an ancient Greek warrior, presumably the mythical Queen Hippolyte. This one looked remarkably like Ellena herself.

("I suppose that the artist knew on which side her bread is buttered," sneered Fenella.)

Ellena's speech was an impassioned one. She appealed to all citizens to support her in the defense of law and order. She left no doubt in the minds of her audience as to who was the chief upholder of law and order on New Sparta. At the finish, almost as an afterthought, she did mention her missing husband and assured everybody that until his return the business of government was in good hands.

After she finished talking there was a brief coverage of the attack on the Palace and an assurance that the ringleaders of what was referred to as a riot were under arrest. There was no mention of casualties.

Sufficient unto the day, thought Grimes, was the evil thereof. No doubt the morrow would bring its own evils. He decided to go outside, onto the balcony, to smoke a quiet pipe before retiring.

The night seemed to be quiet enough. There were no sounds of gunfire, near or distant. There was no wailing of sirens. Somebody, somewhere not too far away, was plucking at a stringed instrument, accompanying a woman who was softly, not untunefully singing. Grimes did not recognize the song. Of one thing he was sure; it was a very old one. He looked up at the sky, at the stars, at the constellations. These had been named by the first colonists, all of them after gods and heroes of Greek mythology. Poseidon and Cyclops, Jason and Ulysses, Ares and Hercules . . . There were no female names. Would Ellena, Grimes wondered, order her tame astronomers to rectify this? Would the spectacular grouping now called Ares be renamed Hippolyte?

He was still staring upward when something whirred past his right ear, striking the window frame behind him with a clatter. At once he dropped on to all fours, seeking the protection, such as it was, of the ornamental rail enclosing the balcony. But there were no further missiles.

He heard Maggie ask sharply, "What was that?" and Fenella demand, "What are you *doing*, Grimes? Praying? Are you sure that Mecca's that way?"

"Down, you silly bitches!" he snarled. "Don't make targets of yourselves!"

"Targets?" echoed Maggie.

He crawled around to face them.

"Get inside!" he ordered. "Away from the window! Somebody's throwing things at us . . ."

"Only a boomerang," said Maggie. "A *little* boomerang. It couldn't hurt a fly . . ." She had picked up the small crescent of cunningly carved wood and was examining it. "There's writing on it . . ."

Grimes got to his feet, took the thing from Maggie. On the flat side of it, in childishly formed capitals, was a brief message. BRASIDUS HELD PRISONER AT MELITUS. There was no signature. In lieu there was the figure of a familiar animal.

"What the hell is that supposed to be?" asked Maggie. "A dinosaur?"

"A kangaroo, of course," said Grimes. "And this primitive airmail letter is from Shirl or Darleen, or both of them. They've been keeping their ears flapping."

They all went back inside. Grimes got out the large atlas. He found Melitus without any trouble. Both a small mountain and a village on its western slopes had that name. It was wild country, with no towns or cities, no roads or railways, only the occasional village, only goat tracks running from nowhere much to nowhere at all. It would be accessible enough to the dirigibles of Trans-Sparta Airlines, or to those of the Spartan Navy, or to any form of heavier-than-air transport.

"But," said Grimes, "*we* don't have wings."

"Lieutenant Gupta and his *Krait* are under my orders," said Maggie. "Under *your* orders actually, although he's not supposed to know that."

"And just how," asked Grimes, "are we going to give Gupta any orders?"

"You'll think of a way," said Maggie. "You always do."

"And meanwhile," grumbled Fenella, "dear Ellena will tighten her grip on this planet. Oh, I don't particularly mind. All in all, women make no more of a balls of running things than men do. As long as I get my exclusive story. . . ."

"Is that all you ever think of?" flared Maggie. "A story? Brasidus is our friend. Too, until and unless the Federation decides otherwise, he is the recognized ruler of this world."

"All right. All right. But don't forget that I'm playing along with you two only because I scent a story."

They turned in then.

Grimes and Maggie did not go to sleep at once. Neither did they talk much. They decided that any long-range planning was out of the question and that, meanwhile, they would make the best of what time they had together.

The next morning breakfast, such as it was, was served to them in Grimes' sitting room. Muddy coffee and little, sweet rolls were not, he thought and said, a solid foundation upon which to build the day. Fenella and Maggie were inclined to agree with him. Before they had quite finished the meal Lieutenant Phryne came in, saying that she had orders to escort them to the Lady Ellena's presence. She refused to tell them what they were wanted for.

Ellena received them in her command headquarters. She was wearing the uniform of a high-ranking Amazon officer. In an odd sort of way it suited her even though her body was not shown to advantage by a costume that was, essentially, an affair of leather straps, brass buckles and a short kilt. She was seated behind a desk the surface of which was dominated by her highly polished, plumed, bronze helmet. There was barely room for the papers—reports, possibly—which she had been studying. On the walls were illuminated maps—of the city, of the surrounding countryside, of the entire planet. There was communications equipment elaborate enough to handle the needs of a small army. (It was handling the needs of such an army.) Female officers were doing things at the consoles before which they were sitting, speaking, low-voiced, into microphones.

"The prisoners, Ma'am," announced Phryne smartly.

"Not prisoners, Lieutenant," Ellena corrected her. "The guests. My husband's guests." She looked up from her papers. "Good morning, Commodore. Commander, Miz Prune. Please be seated." Phryne brought them hard chairs. "You will recall that yesterday we discussed the possibility of putting the Survey Service's courier *Krait* at the disposal of the civil power on this planet. . . ."

The civil *power*? wondered Grimes, looking around at the uniformed, armed women, at a screen on one of the walls which had come to life showing a small squadron of Amazon chariots proceeding along a city street, spraying the buildings on either side with heavy machine-gun fire.

"I am not so sure, Lady," said Maggie, "that this would be advisable. It has occurred to me that *Krait* would be better employed in the protection of Federation interests—the shipping in the spaceport, for example . . ."

"I could, I suppose," said Ellena coldly, "invoke the Right of Angary. . . ."

A space-lawyer yet! thought Grimes. But had the Right of Angary ever been invoked to justify the seizure of a ship of war rather than that of a mere merchantman? An interesting legal point . . . Anyhow, he decided suddenly, *he* wanted *Krait*, with, but preferably without, her rightfully appointed captain. After all he, in his younger days, had commanded such a vessel.

He pulled out his pipe, began to fill it. It was an invaluable aid to thinking.

"Put that thing away, Commodore," ordered Ellena.

"As you wish, Lady." He turned to Maggie. "I think, Commander Lazenby, that the Lady Ellena is well within her rights. And, surely, it is in the interests of the Federation, of which New Sparta is a member, that every effort be made to put a stop to civil commotion which might well develop into a civil war."

"Commodore Grimes," said Ellena, "has far more experience in such matters than you do, Commander Lazenby. After all, he has been a planetary ruler himself."

"I bow," said Maggie, "to the superior knowledge of the Archon's wife and the ex-Governor."

Fenella made a noise that could have been either a snort or a snigger.

Ellena glared at the two offworld women and favored Grimes with an almost sweet smile—but her eyes were cold and calculating.

"Then, Commodore," she said, "would you mind persuading Commander Lazenby to order *Krait*'s captain to lift ship at once and proceed forthwith to the Palace? I am no expert in these matters but I imagine that such a small spacecraft will be able to make a landing on the Amazons' drill ground."

"There's enough room there," said Grimes, "for a Constellation Class cruiser, provided she's handled with care. A Serpent Class courier could set down on the front lawn of the average suburban villa."

"You are the expert. Lieutenant Phryne, please see to it that an outside communications channel is made available to Commander Lazenby. Get through to the *Krait*'s captain."

Phryne went to one of the consoles against the wall. She punched buttons. The screen came alive. The face of a Federation Survey Service ensign—the single stripe of gold braid on each of his shoulderboards denoted his rank—appeared.

"*Krait* here," he said.

"Lieutenant Phryne of the Amazon Guard here, speaking from the Palace for the Lady Ellena. Call your captain to the phone, please."

"But what business. . . ."

"The Lady Ellena's business. Hurry!"

The young man vanished. In the screen were depicted surroundings that had once been very familiar to Grimes, the interior of the cramped control room of a Serpent Class courier. Since his time, he thought, there had been very few changes in layout. That was all to the good.

Lieutenant Gupta's thin brown face appeared in the screen.

"Captain of *Krait* here," he said.

"Commander Lazenby here," said Maggie, who had taken Phryne's place facing the screen.

"Yes, Commander?" Then, "Can you tell me what is happening? I sent Lieutenant Hale, my PCO, ashore to mingle with the people to find out what he could, but he has not yet returned . . ."

"PCO?" whispered Ellena to Grimes.

"Psionic Communications Officer," he whispered in reply. "A trained telepath. Carried these days by Survey Service ships more for espionage than for communicating over light-years. . . ."

And so the mind-reader isn't aboard, he thought. *So much the better.*

"Lieutenant Gupta," asked Maggie, "are you ready for lift-off?"

"Of course, Commander."

"I have orders for you, Lieutenant. You are to proceed forthwith to the Palace, to place yourself at the disposal of the New Spartan government."

"I question your authority, Commander. May I remind you that you are an officer of the Scientific Branch, not of the Spaceman Branch?"

"And may I remind you, Lieutenant, that prior to our departure from Port Woomera, on Earth, you were told, in my presence and the presence of your officers, by no less a person than Rear Admiral Damien, that while on New Sparta you were to consider yourself under my orders?"

"That is so," admitted Gupta grudgingly. "Even so, I would remind you that this conversation is being recorded."

"So bloody what?" exploded Maggie. "Just get here, that's all, or I'll see to it that Admiral Damien has your guts for garters."

"But. . . ."

"Just get here, that's all."

"But where shall I land?" Gupta asked plaintively.

"Tell him," said Grimes, "that beacons will be set out in the middle of the Amazons' drill ground."

"Was that Commodore Grimes?" demanded Gupta.

"It was," said Grimes. "It is."

"May Vishnu preserve me!" muttered Gupta.

Chapter 23

Amazingly and extremely fortunately Grimes was able to get some time alone with Maggie and Fenella. Somehow he had been put in charge of setting up makeshift spaceport facilities in the drill ground, with Amazons scurrying hither and yon at his bidding. Among these women soldiers were Shirl and Darleen. Grimes called them to him, on the pretense that they were to act as his liaison with the Amazon officer in charge.

"Did you get our note?" asked one of the New Alicians.

"Of course. It was the information I needed. Now, you two, stick close to us . . ." He broke off the conversation to give orders to an Amazon sergeant. "Yes. I want that inertial drive pinnace out of the way. The field must be completely cleared." And to a lieutenant, "Just leave it here, will you? Yes, I can operate it . . ." From the speaker of the portable transceiver came a voice, that of Lieutenant Gupta. "*Krait* to Palace, *Krait* to Palace. Do you read me? Over." Shirl handed Grimes the microphone on its long lead. "Palace to *Krait*," he said. "I read you loud and clear. Over." "Lifting off," came the reply. "Are you ready for me? Over." "Not quite. I shall call you as soon as the marker beacons are set out. Over and out."

He was free now to give hasty instructions to the four women. "Gupta is under *your* orders, Maggie. I want him and all his people out of the ship. You go aboard on some pretext—to the control room. You know how to operate the airlock controls, don't you? Good. Then, as soon as we get the chance, the rest of us will board. Button up as soon as we've done so and get upstairs in a hurry. You can do that much, can't you? Then I'll take over as soon as I can."

"What if we're fired on while we're lifting?" she asked. "I'm no fighter pilot. I'm only a simple scientist with the minimal training in ship handling required for all Survey Service officers in the non-spaceman branches."

"*Krait*'s a Federation ship. I don't think that Ellena would dare to try to blast her out of the sky. At least, I hope not. And I'll scamper up to control, to take over, as soon as I possibly can."

And then, leaving Maggie and Fenella standing by the transceiver, he, with Shirl and Darleen as his aides, took charge of the final preparations for the reception of the courier. Three powerful blinker lights had been found and adjusted to throw their beams upward and set out in a triangle almost at the exact center of the field. The lights were not the regulation scarlet but an intense blue. It did not matter. Gupta would be told what to expect.

Gupta had made good time, drifting over from the spaceport on lateral thrust. The arrhythmic cacophony of his inertial drive was beating down from the clear sky as he hung over the drill ground at an altitude of one kilometer. The light of the mid-morning sun was reflected dazzlingly from her sleek slimness.

"Clear the field!" Grimes bellowed through a borrowed bullhorn.

"Clear the field!" the cry was taken up by officers and NCOs.

Grimes, accompanied by Shirl and Darleen, returned to the transceiver. He took the microphone from Maggie, ordered Gupta to land at the position marked by the beacons. Gupta acknowledged, then came in slowly, very slowly. Anyone would think, thought Grimes, that *Krait* had been built from especially fragile eggshells.

But *Krait* came in, her inertial drive hammering, maintaining her in a condition of almost weightlessness. Luckily there was no wind; had there been she would have been blown all over the field like a toy balloon.

She came in, and she landed. Her drive was not shut off but was left running, muttering irritably to itself, in neutral. Obviously Lieutenant Gupta wasn't at all happy about the situation. Grimes was. *Krait*, even under Maggie's unskilled management, would be able to make a quick get-away.

"*Krait* to Commander Lazenby," came from the transceiver speaker. "Your orders, please?"

Grimes passed the microphone to Maggie. "Report to the Lady Ellena in the command office, please."

There was another period of waiting.

At last *Krait*'s airlock door opened and the ramp was extended. Down it marched Lieutenant Gupta. For some reason he had taken the time to change into his full dress finery—starched white linen, frock coat, gold-braided sword belt and ceremonial sword in gold-braided scabbard, gold-trimmed fore-and-aft hat. He threw a grudging salute in Maggie's general direction. She, not in uniform, could not reply in kind but bowed slightly and stiffly.

"Where are your officers, Lieutenant?" asked Maggie.

"At their stations still, Commander."

"They are to accompany you to audience with the Lady Ellena. It is essential that her instructions be heard by everybody."

"If you so wish," said Gupta. He lifted his right wrist to his lips to speak into the communicator.

"Tell them," said Maggie, "not to bother to change out of working uniform. They can come just as they are."

"*All* the officers?" queried Gupta.

"Yes."

"But regulations require that there must be a shipkeeper."

She said, "I shall be your shipkeeper until you return. In any case, I wish to get some things from my cabin."

Scowling, Gupta barked orders into his communicator.

They came down the ramp in their slate gray shorts-and-shirt working uniform—a lieutenant jg, three ensigns, first lieutenant, navigator, electronicist and engineer officer. This latter, Grimes noted happily, had not shut down the drive before leaving the ship. He hoped that Gupta would not send him back to do so. But Gupta, unlike Grimes when he had been captain of such a vessel, was a slave to regulations. In these circumstances the drive must be left running until such time as the captain decided that it was safe to immobilize his command. And he was leaving *Krait* in the hands of an officer—Commander Lazenby—senior to himself.

Lieutenant Phryne marched up to them, followed by six Amazon privates. She saluted with drawn sword.

"Lieutenant," said Maggie, "please escort these gentlemen to the Lady Ellena."

"As you say, Commander."

As *Krait*'s people marched off, Maggie mounted the ramp, passed through the airlock doors. How long would it take her to get up to control? Grimes had timed himself many years ago; it was one of the emergency drills. He doubted that she would break his record. He had done it in just under five minutes—but he had known the layout of the ship. Should he allow Maggie double that time? He snuck a glance at his wrist companion, surreptitiously adjusted and switched on the alarm. He looked around the drill ground. The well-disciplined Amazons had been ordered to clear the field; that order still stood. They were standing there around the perimeter, sunlight brilliantly reflected from metal accoutrements. Even so, Grimes thought, he and the others would have to be fast. Those women were dead shots and in the event of their being ordered to use no firearms, to take their prisoners alive, they could *run*.

His wrist companion suddenly *beeped*.

"Now!" barked Grimes.

Fenella sprinted up the ramp. Shirl and Darleen each made it to the airlock with a single leap. Grimes followed hard on their heels. He was dimly aware that the Amazons had broken ranks, were pouring inwards from all sides toward the little spaceship. But he had no time to watch them. The outer airlock door was shutting, was shut. The deck under his feet lurched. He and Fenella and Shirl and Darleen were thrown into a huddle. Structural members were either singing or rattling, or both. Maggie must have slammed the drive straight from neutral to maximum lift.

He disentangled himself from the women, began the laborious climb—it seemed as though he were having to fight at least two gravities—up the spiral staircase, from the airlock to control.

Chapter 24

He pulled himself up through the hatch into the control compartment.

Maggie was hunched in the captain's chair, staring at the read-out screens before her, at the display of flickering numerals that told their story of ever- and rapidly increasing altitude.

Grimes made his way to the first lieutenant's seat with its duplicate controls, flopped into it with a sigh of relief.

"All right, Maggie," he said. "I'll take over."

"You'd better," she told him. "I've been wondering what to do next."

"You've done very well so far," he said. "You got us out of there very nicely."

He reduced thrust to a reasonable level. *Krait* was still climb-ing but now people could move about inside her hull at some-thing better than a crawl, not hampered by a doubling of their body weight. He then gave his attention to the screens giving him views in all directions. He was half expecting that there would be pursuit of some kind but there was not.

"What now?" asked Maggie. "Do we go to Melitus to rescue Brasidus?"

"Not yet," said Grimes. "We carry on straight up. It may fool Ellena, it may not. I hope it does." He chuckled. "Let's try this scenario on for size. The notorious pirate, John Grimes, aided by his female accomplices, feloniously seized the Federation Survey Service's courier *Krait*. . . ."

"And why would he do that? And why should Commander Lazenby, of all people, help him? To say nothing of Fenella Prune and Shirl and Darleen. . . ."

"We'll get Fenella to write the script. You and Shirl and Darleen are hopelessly in love with me, slaves of passion. And Fenella's just along for the ride, getting material for her next piece in Star Scandals."

She laughed. "You could do her job as well as she does. But this scenario of yours. . . . There was opportunity for you to carry out your piratical act. You seized it. But what was the motive? I am assuming that Ellena does not know that *we* know where Brasidus is being held."

"Mphm." Grimes filled and lit his pipe. "But, before we start kicking ideas around to see if they yelp, let's get the others up here." He spoke into a microphone. "This is the captain speaking. All hands to report to the control room. On the double."

"Where *is* the control room?" came Fenella's yelp from the intercom speaker.

"Just follow the spiral staircase up as far as you can go."

"Isn't there an elevator?"

"This," said Grimes, "is a Serpent Class courier, not a Constellation Class cruiser."

"Even an Epsilon Class star tramp has an elevator in the axial shaft!" she snapped.

"Stop arguing!" he yelled. "Just get up here!"

She did, without overmuch delay, accompanied by Shirl and Darleen. There were chairs for only two of the newcomers but Darleen, squatting on the deck, did not appear to be too uncomfortable.

Grimes talked.

"This is the way that I see things. I'm an outsider who just happens to have come to New Sparta at a time when all manner of balloons are going up. I came to New Sparta to wait there for the arrival of my ship, *Sister Sue,* which vessel is all my worldly wealth. I have heard rumors that the New Spartan government intends to seize her, for conversion to an auxiliary cruiser. (Well, Ellena could do that, if she had the brains to think of it. She wouldn't dare to seize a ship belonging to one of the major lines.) So, not for the first time in my career, I'm playing the game according to *my* rules.''

"I'll say you are!" exclaimed Fenella. "You always keep telling us that you were never a pirate, but what you've just done bears all the earmarks of piracy."

"Never mind that. But there's one crime that I have committed—I've lifted from New Sparta without first obtaining Outward Clearance. Even so, as far as Aerospace Control is concerned *Krait* was put at the disposal of the New Spartan government. It doesn't much matter. All the legalities and illegalities can be sorted out later."

"Oh, we all of us know that the Law is an ass, Grimes," said Fenella impatiently. "Just what are your intentions, legal or otherwise?"

"To begin with, a spot of misdirection. As soon as we're clear of the atmosphere I'll switch to Mannschenn Drive, as though at the commencement of a Deep Space voyage. And then I'll attempt to raise *Sister Sue* on Carlotti Radio. Of necessity it will be a broad beam transmission; I don't know where she is, only the general direction from which she will be approaching. My signals will be monitored on New Sparta."

"And what will you tell *Sister Sue*?" asked Maggie.

"I'll try to arrange a rendezvous with her, about one light-year—no, not 'about,' exactly—from New Sparta. I shall tell Williams that he is, on no account, to approach any closer and that I shall be boarding to take command."

"Won't your Mr. Williams—or Captain Williams as he still is—think that these orders are rather . . . weird?" asked Fenella.

"Probably. But he should be used to weird orders by this time."

Krait drove up through the last tenuous shreds of atmosphere, through the belts of charged particles. Aerospace Control began, at last, to take an interest in her.

"Aerospace Control to *Krait* . . . Aerospace Control to *Krait*. . . ."

"*Krait* to Aerospace Control," said Grimes into the microphone. "I read you loud and clear."

"Return at once to the spaceport, *Krait*."

"Negative," said Grimes.

After that he ignored the stream of orders and threats that poured from the NST transceiver speaker.

It was time then to actuate the Mannschenn Drive. The rotors in their intricate array began to spin, tumbling, precessing, warping the dimensions of normal Space-Time around themselves and the ship. Perspective was distorted, colors sagged down the spectrum and what few orders Grimes gave were as though uttered in an echo chamber. But, as sometimes was the case, there were no *déjà vu* phenomena, no flashes of precognition.

And then it was over.

Krait was falling through a blackness against which the stars were no longer points of light but vague, slowly writhing nebulosities.

"So that's that," said Maggie practically.

"That's that," agreed Grimes. "Now all I have to do is to get the bold Billy on the blower and tell him my pack of lies, for Ellena's benefit."

In its own little compartment the Mobius Strip antenna of the Carlotti Deep Space Radio was revolving and its signals, on broad beam, were being picked up, instantaneously, by every receiver within their range, which was a very distant one—and being picked up, reciprocally, by Aerospace Control on New Sparta.

"Grimes to *Sister Sue*," said Grimes. "Grimes to *Sister Sue*. Do you read me?"

At last there came a reply in a male voice strange to Grimes, faint, as though coming from a very long way off—which it was.

"*Sister Sue* here. Pass your message."

"Who is that speaking?" asked Grimes.

"The third officer. Pass your message."

"Get Captain Williams for me, please."

"He's sleeping. I'm perfectly capable of taking your message."

"Get Captain Williams for me. Now."

"*Who* is that calling?"

"Grimes."

"Is that the name of a ship or some fancy acronym?"

"Grimes," repeated the owner of that name. "John Grimes. The owner. Your employer. Get Captain Williams to the Carlottiphone *at once*."

"How do I know that you're Grimes?"

"You should know by this time, young man, that not any Tom, Dick or Harry can get access to a Carlotti transceiver. Get Captain Williams for me. And see if you can arrange a visual hook-up as well as audio. I've the power here to handle it."

"Oh, all right, all right. Sir."

Williams wasted no time coming to *Sister Sue*'s control room. His cheerful, fleshy face appeared in the screen.

"Oh, it is you, Skipper. What's the rush? Couldn't it all have waited until I set her down on New Sparta?"

"It couldn't, Billy."

"But you were always getting on to me about the expense of needless Carlotti communications . . ."

"This one is not needless. To begin with, New Sparta's in a state of upheaval. The Archon was kidnapped and his wife, the Lady Ellena, took over the government. Now she seems to have a civil war on her hands. I don't want my ship sitting on her arse at Port Sparta with shooting going on all about her."

"She's been shot at before, Skipper."

"There's nothing more annoying," said Grimes, "than being shot at in somebody else's war. I want you to heave to, a light-year out, until the dust settles. I'll rendezvous with you and come aboard to talk things over."

"Where are you calling from, Skipper?" asked Williams. "Have you got yourself another ship? Who are those popsies in the background?"

"Yes, I have borrowed a ship. Never mind from whom. And I'm on my way out to you now. I'll home on your Carlotti broadcast. I've good equipment here."

"I'll be waiting for you, Skipper."

"Give my regards to Magda, will you? And to old Mr. Stewart."

"Willco, Skipper."

"See you," said Grimes. "Out."

Yes, he would be seeing Williams, but not for a while yet.

Chapter 25

Krait, insofar as New Sparta Aerospace Control was concerned, was now an invisible ship, falling through the warped dimensions toward her rendezvous with *Sister Sue*, undetectable by radar as long as her Mannschenn Drive was in operation. Some planets—such worlds as were considered to be strategically important—had defense satellites in orbit crammed with sophisticated equipment, such as long-range Mass Proximity Indicators capable of picking up approaching vessels running under Mannschenn Drive. New Sparta was not strategically important.

So while the Lady Ellena would be more than a little annoyed by the theft of a minor warship that she had hoped to acquire for her own use she might well be pleased, thought Grimes, at the removal from her domain of three nuisances—Maggie Lazenby, Fenella Pruin and Grimes himself. He allowed himself to feel sorry for Lieutenant Gupta. He and his officers, spacemen without a spaceship, would be discovering that they were far from welcome guests in the Palace. . . .

Meanwhile it was time that he started thinking of his own strategy rather than the troubles of others. He would begin by setting an orbital course for Melitus rather than trajectory for *Sister Sue*'s estimated position. Just where was Melitus?

He and the women went down to the wardroom—*Krait* was quite capable of looking after herself—where there was a playmaster which, like any such device aboard a spaceship, could be used to obtain information from the library bank. They all took seats, Grimes in one from which he could operate the playmaster's controls. He punched for LIBRARY, then for PLANETARY INFORMATION, then for NEW SPARTA, then for MELITUS. Words appeared on the screen. *Mountain, 1.7 kilometers above sea level, Latitude 37°14′ S., Longitude 176°59′ E.*

Village called Melitus? typed Grimes.

No information, appeared the reply.

Map of Mount Melitus vicinity?
Not in library bank.

Grimes swore. "I should," he said, "have brought along the atlas from my quarters."

"It would have looked suspicious," said Fenella, "if you'd been carrying it around with you."

"I could have torn out one or two relevant pages," said Grimes, "and put them in my pockets."

"But you didn't," said Fenella.

"There are some maps in my cabin," Maggie told them. "I'll get them now."

She spread them on the wardroom table. Grimes found the one he wanted, studied it carefully. When making his final approach, back in normal Space-Time, he would be shielded by the bulk of the planet from the probing radar of Aerospace Control. Unluckily he would be unable to make a quiet approach; the inertial drive unit of even a small ship is noisy; the only really heavy sonic insulation is to protect the eardrums of the crew. But there was a technique which he might employ, that he would employ if conditions were suitable. It was one that he had read about but had never seen used.

The map was a contour one. To the north Mount Melitus was steep, in parts practically sheer cliff. The southern face was sloped almost gently to the plain. There was a river, little more than a stream, that had its source about halfway up the mountain. A little below this source was the village of Melitus. But those contour lines. . . . The southern slopes were only comparatively gentle but there did not seem to be any suitable place upon which to set down a spaceship, even a small one. Grimes studied the map more carefully, took a pair of dividers to measure off distances. The river made a horseshoe bend just over a kilometer downstream from the village. The almost-island so formed was devoid of contour lines. Did that mean anything or was it no more than slovenly cartography? But the map, saw Grimes, was a Survey Service publication and the Survey Service's cartographers prided themselves on their thoroughness. He hoped they had been thorough when charting the Mount Melitus area.

He said, "You know something of the layout of the ship, Maggie. See if you can rustle up some kind of a meal. Sandwiches will do. Shirl and Darleen—you're army officers. . . ."

They laughed at that.

"But you know something about weapons," he went on. "You must have received some instruction when you were in the Amazon Guard as well as dishing it out. Go through the ship and collect all the lethal ironmongery you can find and bring it here, to the wardroom. And you, Fenella, make rounds of the officers' cabins and the storerooms and find clothing, for all of us, suitable for an uphill hike through rough country.

"I shall be going back to Control." He rolled up the map that he had been studying, took it with him. "You know where to find me if you want me."

Maggie brought him his sandwiches—rather inferior ham with not enough mustard—and a vacuum flask of coffee that was only a little better than the brew which they had become used to (but never liked) in the Palace. But he did not complain. (As far as Maggie was concerned he had learned, long since, that it was unwise to do so.) He munched stolidly while keeping a watchful eye on the instruments. One drawback of making an orbit around a planet with the ship's Mannschenn Drive in operation is that there are no identifiable landmarks; the appearance of a world viewed in such conditions has been described as that of a Klein Flask blown by a drunken glassblower.

But the instruments, Grimes hoped, were not lying.

"What time—local time, that is—should we get there?" asked Maggie.

"Midnight," replied Grimes. "Anyhow, that's what I've programed the little bitch for. How are the girls getting on with their fossicking?"

"Fenella's found clothing for all of us—tough coveralls. Boots might be a problem. Shirl and Darleen have rather long feet, as probably you've already noticed."

"On their own planet," he said, "they're used to running around barefoot. What about rainwear?"

"Rainwear? Are you expecting rain?"

"Rain has been known to fall," he said. "Tell Fenella, when you go back down, to find something suitable. And the weapons?"

"So far a stungun, fully charged, with belt and holster, for each of us. Laser pistols likewise. And projectile pistols."

He said, "We can't load ourselves down with too much. We'll take the stunguns and the lasers. We don't want to do any killing."

"Lasers kill people. Or hadn't you noticed?"

"A laser is a tool as well as a weapon, Maggie. It comes in handy for burning through doors, for example. Too, it's silent. Even more so than a stungun."

"Shirl and Darleen have their own ideas about silent weapons," she said.

"What do you mean?"

"They found a dozen metal discs—what they're *for* the Odd Gods alone know!—in the engineer's workshop. They say that once they're given a cutting edge they'll be very nice throwing weapons."

Grimes muttered something about bloodthirsty little bitches.

"I thought that you liked them, John," said Maggie.

"I do. But. . . ."

"Haven't you ever shed any blood during your career?"

"Yes. But. . . ."

But what he did not tell her was that he strongly suspected that the guards at Miletus, Ellena's people, would be women. He derided himself for his old-fashioned ideas but still was reluctant to kill a member of the opposite sex.

Chapter 26

Krait made her return to normal Space-Time, began her descent to the surface of New Sparta, to Mount Melitus. Maggie and Fenella were with Grimes in the control room; Maggie was there as a sort of co-pilot—after all, as a Survey Service officer, although not in the Spaceman Branch, she knew something about ship-handling—and Fenella was, as always, just getting into everything. Grimes had succeeded in persuading Shirl and Darleen to busy themselves elsewhere. Much as he liked them both this was an occasion when he could do without their distracting chatter.

As the little ship dropped to the nightside hemisphere greater and greater detail was displayed in the stern view radar screen, in three-dimensional presentation. There was Mount Melitus, almost directly below *Krait*. Grimes applied a touch of lateral thrust so that the mountain was now to the south of the line of descent. Its hulking mass, he explained, would shield the village on the southern slopes from the clangor of the inertial drive.

"But our landing place," objected Fenella, "*is* on the southern slopes. They're bound to hear us sooner or later—and soon enough to be ready and waiting for us.''

"Not necessarily," Grimes told her.

He made adjustments to the radar controls, increasing sensitivity. Clouds were now visible in the screen. The wind, as it should have been at this time of year, as he had hoped that it would be, was from the north, blowing over the relatively warm Aegean Sea on to the land, striking the sheer, northern face of the mountain and being deflected upward into cooler atmospheric levels.

He checked the state of readiness of the missile projector. It was loaded. He had seen to that himself. In the tube was a rocket with a Mark XXV Incendiary warhead. It was one of the viler anti-personnel weapons, one that Grimes, during his Survey Service days, had hoped that he would never have to use. Now he was going to use it—although not directly against personnel.

"Who are you going to shoot at?" asked Fenella interestedly. "I thought that the object of this exercise was to rescue Brasidus, not to blow him to pieces."

"*What*, not *who*," said Grimes. "I'm looking for a nice, fat cloud. One that's just skimming the peak of the mountain on its way south."

"Looking for a *cloud*? Are you out of your tiny mind?"

"The Commodore knows what he's doing!" snapped Maggie. Then, "By the way, what are you doing?"

He laughed.

"I'm going to use a technique that was used, some years ago, on Bolodrin. A non-aligned planet, of no great importance, but one which both the Shaara and ourselves would like to draw within our spheres of influence. A humanoid population. An export trade of agricultural products. Well, there had been a quite disastrous planet-wide drought. One of our ships—the Zodiac Class cruiser *Scorpio*—was there showing the flag. The Tronmach—it translates roughly to Hereditary President—appealed to the captain of *Scorpio*, as the representative of a technologically superior culture, to Do Something about the drought. Captain Samson went into a huddle with his scientific officers. They decided to seed likely cloud formations. With Hell Balls.''

"What's a Hell Ball?" asked Fenella.

"What my missile projector is loaded with. It's the pet name for the Mark XXV Incendiary Device, one of the more horrid anti-personnel weapons. Imagine an expanding vortex of plasma, superheated, electrically hyperactive gases. . . .''

"And did this bright idea work?"

"Too well. The drought was broken all right. Rivers burst their banks. Hailstorms flattened orchards. If the Shaara had grabbed the opportunity, sending ships with all manner of aid, Bolodrin would have happily become an Associate Hive Member. But they were slow off the mark and the Federation organized relief expenditures. Nonetheless relations were strained and Captain Samson suffered premature retirement. Mphm. Looks like a suitable target coming up now. . . . Range about fifty kilometers. . . ."

He busied himself at the fire control console, aligning the projector, setting the fuse of the warhead.

He pushed the button.

Only faintly luminous, the exhaust of the rocket was almost invisible.

The slow explosion of the warhead was not. In the center of the towering cumulus bright flame burgeoned and lightnings writhed, wreathing the mountain peak with lambent fire, lashing out to other cloud formations. A clockwise rotation seemed already to have been initiated, a cyclonic vortex. It was the birth of a hurricane.

Grimes could imagine what the conditions would soon be on the southern slopes of Melitus, the country normally protected from extremes of weather by the bulk of the mountain. There would be torrential rain and shrieking winds and a continuous cannonade of thunder and lightning, an uproar among which the arrhythmic clangor of a small ship's inertial drive unit would go unnoticed.

He hoped.

With the controls now on manual he continued his descent. He skimmed the peak with less clearance than he had intended; a vicious downdraft caught *Krait* and had he not reacted swiftly, slamming on maximum lift, the ship must surely have been wrecked.

Then he was over the mountain top, dropping again but not too fast, maintaining a half kilometer altitude from the ground. Sudden gusts buffeted the ship, tilting her from the vertical. A fusillade of hail on her skin was audible even through the thick insulation. Nothing, save for the diffused flare of the lightning, could be seen through the viewpoints. Even the radar picture was almost blotted out by storm clutter.

But there was the village. . . .

— And the river. . . .

Grimes followed its course to the horseshoe bend. It looked as it did on the chart. But even if the ground were level, what about trees? There had been no symbols indicating such growths on the map—but trees have a habit of growing over the years. He had hoped to be able to make a visual inspection before landing but, in these conditions, it was impossible.

He hovered almost directly over the almost-island, dropping slowly, keeping *Krait* in position by applications of lateral thrust, this way and that.

"Stand by the viewpoint, Maggie," he ordered. "Yes. That one. If there's a brief clear spell, if the rain lets up, tell me what you see."

"What do you want me to see?"

"What I don't want you to see on our landing place," he said, "is trees. Bushes don't worry me but a large, healthy tree can damage even a big ship sitting down on it!"

"Will do."

And then she was back beside him.

"There was a break, and lightning at the same time. There aren't any trees."

"Landing stations!" ordered Grimes.

Krait sat down hard, dropping the final two meters with her drive in neutral. She sat down hard and she complained, creaking and groaning, rocking on her tripedal landing gear, while shock-absorbers hissed and sighed.

Grimes unbuckled himself from his chair, then led the way out of the control room. In the wardroom Shirl and Darleen were waiting. On the table and on the deck were the articles of clothing that Grimes had specified—the coveralls, the raincapes and the heavy boots. Hanging on the backs of chairs were belts and holstered weapons.

Swiftly the five of them got out of their light clothing, pulled on the coveralls and the heavy boots. Luckily the ship's equipment store had carried a wide range of sizes, so even Shirl and Darleen were shod not too uncomfortably. Grimes packed a rucksack with protective clothing for Brasidus, who would need this for the walk from the village to *Krait*. (Grimes hoped that Brasidus would be able to make the walk, that he would be rescued unharmed.) They belted on the weapons. Shirl and Darleen attached to their belts pouches with clinking contents. Grimes wondered briefly what was in them, then remembered the discs that the two girls had found in the engineer's workshop.

They made their way down the spiral staircase to the airlock, the controls of which had been set to be operated manually.

Grimes was not at all happy about leaving the ship without a duty officer but he had no option. He was the only real spaceperson in the party but, at the same time, he was the obvious leader of the expedition. And all that any of the women could do, if one of them were left in charge, would be to keep a seat in the control room warm.

He and Fenella were first into the airlock chamber. Grimes pushed the button that would open the outer door and, at the same time, extend the telescopic ramp. He was expecting a violent onslaught of wind and rain but his luck, he realized thankfully, was holding. The door was on the lee side of the ship. He adjusted the hood of his raincape, checked the buckles holding the garment about his body, then walked cautiously down the ramp. Away from the ship he began to feel the wind and, even through his layers of clothing, the impact of the huge raindrops. He could hear the thin, high screaming of the wind as it eddied around the metallic tower that was the ship, was blinded by a bolt of lightning that struck nearby and deafened by the *crack!* of the thunder. And what if *Krait* herself should be struck by lightning? Nothing much, he thought (hoped). With her stern vanes well dug into the wet soil she would be well earthed.

He got his eyesight back and turned to look up the ramp. Shirl and Darleen were coming down it and Maggie was silhouetted in the doorway.

"Shut the inner door before you come down!" he yelled.

"What?" he heard her scream.

He repeated the order.

The light behind her diminished as she obeyed him. The airlock chamber itself was only dimly illumined. And then she was following Shirl and Darleen to the ground.

Grimes led the way up the mountainside. There was no possibility of their getting lost; all that they had to do was to keep to the bank of the stream. It was more of a torrent now, swollen by the downpour, roaring and rumbling as displaced boulders, torn from the banks, ground against each other. The wind had almost as much weight as the rushing water, buffeting them as they bent into it, finding its way through the fastenings of their raincapes, ballooning the garments, threatening to lift their wearers from their feet and to send them whirling downhill, airborne flotsam.

The raincapes had to go. Grimes struggled out of his. It was torn from his hands, vanished downwind like a huge, demented bat. The women shed theirs. Maggie, shouting to make herself heard above the wild tumult of wind, water and thunder, made a feeble joke about the willful destruction of Federation property and the necessity thereafter of filling in forms in quintuplicate.

But she could still joke, thought Grimes. Good for her. And the others were bearing up well, even Fenella. No doubt she was thinking in headlines. MY WALK ON THE WILD SIDE.

Bruised and battered by flying debris, deafened by shrieking wind and roaring thunder, blinded by lightning, the party struggled up the mountainside.

And of all the miseries and discomforts the one that Grimes resented most bitterly was the trickle of icy-cold water that found its way through the neckband of his coveralls, meandering down his body to collect in his boots.

Chapter 27

They came at last to the village, such as it was, the huddle of low stone houses, little better than huts most of them, all of them with doors and windows tightly battened against the storm. There was one building, two-storied, larger than the others. From its steeply pitched roof protruded what was obviously a radio communications antenna, a slender mast that whipped as the gusts took hold of it and worried it. It was a wonder that it had survived the storm thus far; not only was there the rain but there was the lightning, stabbing down from the swirling clouds at even the stunted trees that were hardly more than overgrown bushes, exploding them into eruptions of charred splinters.

It had survived thus far; it would be as well, decided Grimes, if it survived for no longer. If Brasidus and his guards were in this house the sooner that means of communication with Sparta City was destroyed the better. He pulled his laser pistol from its holster, tried to take aim at the base of the mast. The wind grabbed his arm and tugged viciously. He tried to use his left hand to steady his right, pressed the firing stud. During a brief, very brief, period of darkness between lightning flashes he saw the beam of intense ruby light, missing the target by meters. He tried again. Maggie tried. Even Fenella tried. The radio mast remained untouched by their fire.

Grimes saw that Shirl was taking one of the metal discs from the pouch at her waist, holding it carefully by the small arc of its circumference that had been left unsharpened. *And what good will that do?* he asked himself scornfully. A thrown missile, launched in the teeth of a howling gale . . . Metal—tough metal admittedly—against metal at least as tough as itself. (That mast must be tough to have survived the storm.)

Shirl stood there, her body swaying in the gusts that assailed her, making no attempt to hold herself rigid as she took aim, not fighting the forces of nature as Grimes and Maggie and Fenella had been trying to do, accommodating herself to them. Her right arm, the hand holding the gleaming disc, went back and then, aided by a wind eddy, snapped forward. Like Grimes and the others, she had been aiming for the base of the mast. Unlike Grimes and the others she might even have hit it. But the disc itself, generating with its swift passage through the heavily charged air a charge of its own, was itself a target. A writhing filament of dazzling incandescence snaked down from the black sky to emmesh the missile, to follow its trajectory even as it was reduced to a coruscation of molten steel.

The disc, what was left of it, would narrowly have missed the base of the mast—but the lightning struck it. Momentarily it took, Grimes thought, the semblance of a Christmas tree, etching its branches and foliage of flame onto his retinas. Slowly he regained his eyesight. Somebody—Maggie—had him by the upper arm, was shaking it.

"John! John!" she was saying, "They're coming out!"

He blinked, then raised his hand to clear the rain from his eyes. A door had opened on the lee side of the building, the side on which they were standing. A figure was standing in the rectangle of yellow light, another one behind it, women both of them.

"I'm not going out in *this*!" Grimes heard faintly.

"Somebody has to. Something has happened to the mast."

"Blown down. Struck by lightning. In this weather anything could happen."

"We have to see what's wrong so we can fix it. Out with you, *now!*"

"Oh, all right. All right."

The smaller of the two women ventured out into the night, picking just the wrong moment for her excursion. A shrieking gust eddied around the house so that even on its lee side there was little protection. Her weatherproof cloak was whipped up over and around her head, blinding her and trapping her arms. She staggered out blindly, her naked legs luminescent in the darkness. She blundered right into the arms of Shirl and Darleen. Her shriek like a hard fist connected with the nape of her neck was muffled by her enveloping garment. She fell to the sodden ground and lay there, face down, her bare rump exposed to the lashing of the driving rain. She would be visible from the open doorway; Grimes and his companions, in their dark clothing, would not.

"Lalia!" the woman standing in the door was screaming. "Lalia! What's wrong? Did you fall?"

And then she had left the shelter of the house, was staggering out over the rough ground, buffeted by the wind, her flimsy robe shredded from her body as she made her unsteady way toward her fallen companion. Grimes and the others withdrew to one side, hoping that they would not be seen, and then, with him in the lead, ran toward the house, their stunguns out and ready. Once inside they slammed and barred the door. (Grimes felt a brief twinge of pity for those two near-naked females shut out in the storm.)

The room in which they were standing was sparsely furnished—a rough table, a half dozen equally rough chairs, a pressure lantern hanging from a rafter. Against the far wall a wooden staircase—more of a ladder really—led to the upper floor. In the side wall to the left was an open doorway.

From it came a female voice.

"Sounds like they're back. Now, perhaps, we'll be able to get this accursed transceiver working again."

"I'm sure that dear Ellena is waiting with bated breath for the rest of our weather report," sneered another female voice.

"Be that as it may, we're still supposed to be in touch every six hours, on the hour, if only to let her know that his sexist lordship is doing as well as may be expected." She raised her voice. "Lalia! Daphne! What's keeping you? Is that aerial still standing?"

Grimes and Maggie, stunguns in hand, advanced to the open door, the others behind them. They saw the four women, who were huddled over the large transceiver upon which they had been working, replacing power cells and printed circuits. One of them he recognized; it was the fat blonde with whom he had tangled on the occasion of the Archon's abduction, although what had been brassy hair was now no more than a gray stubble. There must have been a discharge from the set when the lightning struck and she must have been in the way of it. She looked up from her work and stared at him.

She jumped to her feet, screwdriver in hand.

"You!" she snarled.

"Yes, me," agreed Grimes pleasantly as he shot her.

Beside him Maggie's stungun buzzed as she disposed of two of the other ladies and from behind him Fenella, determined not to be left out of things, loosed off a paralyzing blast at the redhead who was about to throw a spanner at the commodore.

We should have left one of them awake, thought Grimes, *to take us to where they have Brasidus.* Not that it much mattered. This house, little more than a shack, was no castle. There would be very few rooms to search.

They went back into the first room. Somebody was hammering on the door to outside and yelling, "Let us in! Let us in, damn you!"

"Let them in," Grimes whispered to Shirl.

She obeyed.

The two women who had gone to inspect the aerial stumbled in. In normal circumstances they might have been attractive, with what remained of their rain-soaked clothing clinging to quite shapely bodies, but Grimes thought they looked like two drowned rats. They screamed when they saw the intruders, screamed again when the two New Alicians grabbed them, one to each, held them with their arms twisted up painfully behind their backs. Still they stared defiantly at Grimes. One of them spat at him.

"Ladies, ladies," he admonished. Then, with the whipcrack of authority in his voice, "Where is the Archon?"

"Why should we tell you?" growled the taller of the pair.

Grimes raised his stungun in his right hand, with the fingers of his left adjusted the setting.

"John, you're not going to . . . ?" expostulated Maggie. "You said that there was to be no killing."

Grimes hoped that he had the setting right. There was one beam intensity the use of which was supposed to be illegal, against the rules of civilized warfare. It was a matter of very fine adjustment, a fraction of a degree above MAXIMUM STUN although less than LETHAL. Una Freeman, a Federation police officer whom he had once known, had taught him this nasty little trick, telling him that it might come in handy some day. "But be careful," she had warned him. "Overdo it and you'll finish up with a human vegetable who'd be better off dead."

"Where is the Archon?" he demanded again.

"Get stuffed!" came the defiant reply.

Grimes raised the bulky pistol.

"That's right," sneered the woman. "Put me to sleep so I'll never talk. D'you think I don't know a stungun when I see one?"

"Drop her!" Grimes barked to Darleen. "Get away from her!"

For a moment the tall, black-haired woman stood there, then she started toward Grimes, clawlike fingers extended.

Grimes pressed the firing stud.

The weapon whined.

The woman was cut down in mid-leap then fell to the floor, writhing in agony, the muzzle of the pistol still trained on her, still emitting its beam. She was making a shrill grunting noise through her closed mouth and, above this, could be heard the grinding of her teeth. Throughout her body muscle fought against muscle. She was on her back squirming in a ghastly parody of orgasm, and then only her heels and the back of her head were in contact with the floor. Blood trickled from the corners of her mouth.

"Stop!" screamed Maggie.

He released the pressure on the firing stud.

His victim collapsed in a shuddering heap.

"Where is the Archon?" repeated Grimes.

She lifted her head to glare at him. She spat out blood and fragments of broken teeth.

"Get . . . stuffed . . ."

Hating himself, and hating her for being so stubborn, Grimes took aim again.

"I'll tell!" screamed the small, mousy blonde. "I'll tell you! But don't hurt her again!"

"Gutless little bitch!" was all the thanks she got from her friend.

But Grimes felt better when he discovered that his harsh interrogation had been necessary after all. There was a cellar, the trapdoor to which had been concealed by the heavy rug upon which the table had been standing, that could be opened only by pressing a stud, disguised as a nailhead—one among many—in the wooden floor. There was a rough wooden staircase down into the black depths.

"Brasidus!" yelled Grimes into the opening.

"Here!" came the reply from below. Then, "Who's that?"

"Grimes. We've come to get you out!"

But there was something that had to be done first. Grimes set the control knob of his pistol to MEDIUM STUN. He pointed the weapon at the black-haired woman who was still sprawled on the floor, twitching and moaning. He said gently, "This will put you out. You'll feel better when you recover." (It was not quite a lie, although it would be days before the soreness left her overstrained muscles and she would require considerable dental work.)

"Bastard!" she hissed viciously from her bleeding mouth. "Bastard!"

And then she was silent and her body and limbs were no longer twitching.

Darleen lifted the pressure lamp from its bracket, started toward the open trapdoor.

"Hold it!" ordered Grimes. "Let *her* go first." He hustled the small blonde toward the head of the stairway. "There may be booby traps."

So they followed their prisoner down into what was more of a cellar than a real dungeon, smelling of the wine and the spicy foodstuffs stored therein, although in one corner there was a cage constructed from stout metal bars, its door secured by a heavy padlock. In this stood Brasidus. He was naked and his beard and hair were unkempt but otherwise he seemed in good enough condition.

"John!" he cried. "Maggie! By all the gods, it's good to see you!"

"And good to see you!" said Grimes. He grabbed the small blonde by her shoulder. "Where's the key to this cage?"

"I . . . I don't know. . . ."

"Give her the same treatment that you gave the other bitch," suggested Fenella viciously.

But Maggie had returned her stungun to its holster, pulled out her laser pistol. An acrid stink of burning metal filled the air and incandescent, molten gobbets hissed and crackled as they fell to the floor.

Free, Brasidus hugged the embarrassed Grimes in a bearlike embrace, then did the same to Maggie. ("Don't *I* get a kiss?" complained Fenella.) And then, amazingly, he swept the small blonde into his arms, pressed his lips on hers. She did not resist, in fact cooperated quite willingly.

"Might I ask," inquired Fenella, "just what the hell is going on here?"

Brasidus laughed. "It's because of Lalia that I'm down in this hole. At first I enjoyed considerably more freedom. Lalia and I

. . . . Oh, well, you know how things are. Daphne caught us at it . . ."

"Perhaps Daphne had the right to be jealous," suggested Fenella.

"It's time that we were getting out of here," said Grimes. "I've a ship waiting."

"Come, then," said Brasidus. With his arm still about Lalia's shoulders he started for the foot of the staircase.

"You aren't taking *her* with you," stated rather than asked Fenella.

"Why not? She was good to me."

And good to Daphne, thought Grimes, *and, above all, good to herself.*

He said, "I'm sorry. She has to stay here."

Brasidus released the girl and shrugged.

"Just as well, perhaps," he muttered. "Probably Ellena wouldn't approve if I brought her into the Palace."

And you've a lot to learn about Ellena, my poor friend, thought Grimes. *But that can wait until we're in the ship on the way back to Port Sparta.*

Maggie's stungun buzzed as she ensured Lalia's unconsciousness for at least half an hour.

Chapter 28

In the upstairs room they gave Brasidus the clothing that they had brought for him, the tough coveralls and the heavy boots. He dressed in sulky silence. They let themselves out of the house. The storm was abating although the rain was still as heavy as ever. There was no longer an almost continuous flare of lightning but laser pistols, set to low intensity, did duty as electric torches to illuminate their way.

The stream whose course they had followed up to the village was now a wild torrent, bearing on its crest all manner of flotsam, uprooted bushes and small trees and the like. Audible even above the sound of rushing water was the grinding rumble of the boulders rolling downhill along the river bed.

But where was *Krait*?

Surely, thought Grimes, *we should be seeing her by now.*

He set the beam of his laser to higher intensity, sent it probing ahead into the rain-lashed darkness. There was a very pretty rainbow effect but no reflection from gleaming metal. He began to feel a growing uneasiness. Surely the little bitch hadn't lifted off by herself . . . Surely some freakish accident, a chance lightning bolt for example, had not caused actuation of the inertial drive machinery. . . .

But that was fantasy.

But where was the ship?

Maggie cried out.

Like Grimes, she had adjusted her laser pistol. Unlike him she was directing the beam only just above ground level. She was first to see the ship. Afterwards it was easy to work out what must have happened, what had happened—the almost-island on which Grimes had set her down had become a real island, an island whose banks were eroded, faster and faster, by the rushing water. With the once-solid ground below her vanes washed away she had toppled. The crash of her falling had just been part of the general tumult of the storm.

Fenella voiced the thoughts of all of them.

"That's fucked it!" she stated.

Too right, thought Grimes, but his mind was working busily. Suppose, just suppose, that the ship's mian machinery had not been too badly damaged . . . Then it would be possible, difficult but possible, to lift her on lateral thrust and then, when high enough from the ground, to turn her about a short axis to a normal attitude. In theory it could be done. In fact Grimes had heard of its being done, although he had never had to attempt such a maneuver himself; the nearest to it had been the righting of a destroyer, a much larger vessel. Then those in the ship had used lateral thrust while he, in control of operations, had employed a spaceyacht as a tug.

But to do anything at all he had to get into the ship.

Accompanied by the others he walked, so far as was possible, around the cigar-shaped hull. It formed a bridge over the river, with the nose on the bank upon which Grimes was standing, with the stern on what little remained of the island. And, Grimes saw by the light of the laser torches, she had fallen in such a way that the airlock was below her. He told Maggie and the others.

"Can't we burn a way in?" she asked. "The control room viewports should be a weak point . . ."

And those viewports, thought Grimes glumly, were supposed to be able to withstand, at least for an appreciable time, the assault of a laser cannon . . . How long would it take hand lasers to make a hole? But it had to be tried.

And so they stood there, the five of them who were armed, with Brasidus watching, aiming their pistols at the center of one of the viewports. Soon their target was obscured by steam as the intense heat vaporized the falling rain, soon the exposed skin of their faces felt as though it were being boiled.

But they persisted.

Then the intense beam of ruby light from Maggie's weapon faded into the infrared, died. She caught the butt of the weapon a clout with her free hand but it did not help. "Power cell's dead," she muttered.

"And mine . . ." said Fenella.

The other lasers sputtered out. The steam dispersed. The eyes of the party became accustomed to the darkness—but, Grimes realized, it was no longer dark. The sun must now be up, somewhere behind the fast-scudding nimbus. He looked at the shallow depression in the thick transparency of the viewport, all that they had been able to achieve at the cost of their most effective weaponry.

He flinched as something whipped past his head with a noise that was part whistle, part crack. A scar of bright metal appeared on the hide of *Krait* just below the viewports. A long time later—it seemed—came the report of a projectile firearm.

"Take cover!" yelled Grimes. "Behind the ship!"

He waited—*like a fool,* he told himself, *like a fool*—until the others had moved, looking toward where he thought the shot had come from, holding his pistol as though for instant use. He saw her, a pale form up the hillside. It was, he thought, the fat blonde. Her body bulk must have minimized the effects of the stungun blast. She had her rifle raised for another shot. It went wild and then she ducked behind a boulder.

Grimes, still holding his useless laser pistol threateningly, walked carefully backward. Just before he joined the others a third shot threw up a fountain of mud by his right foot.

Secure, for the time being, behind the bulk of the crippled courier he said, "There's only one of them. That fat bitch. . . ."

"Hephastia," said Brasidus.

"Thanks," said Grimes. "That saves me the bother of being formally introduced to her. Luckily she doesn't know that our lasers are dead. But when we fail to return her fire she'll realize that they are, and come for us."

"We've the stunguns," said Maggie.

"And what effective range do *they* have?" asked Grimes. "Little more than three meters, if that."

"But how much ammunition does *she* have?" said Fenella.

"We don't know," Grimes told her. "If she's any sort of a shot six rounds should be ample."

Very, very carefully he moved out from behind the protection of the ship, crawling in the mud, keeping head and buttocks well down. He was in time to see a flicker of movement as Hephastia changed positions, scurrying to the cover of another boulder, not appreciably decreasing the range but carrying out an outflanking operation. Even if she were not a member of the Amazon Guard she must have had military training on some world at some time.

He raised his pistol as though about to fire from the prone position. Her retaliatory shot was in line but, luckily for him, over. Frantically he scurried forward, found a boulder of his own behind which to hide. It was by no means as large as he would have wished—and it was even smaller after a well-aimed bullet had reduced the top of it to dust and splinters. Another one reduced it in size still further.

Grimes tried to burrow into the mud while still maintaining some kind of a lookout.

From the corner of his eye he saw movement by the ship.

It was Shirl, walking out calmly, something that gleamed, even in this dull, gray light, in her right hand. It was one of those sharpened discs. Hephastia did not see her. She must have had a one-track mind. With calm deliberation she was whittling away Grimes' little boulder, shot after shot, using some kind of armor-piercing ammunition.

Shirl's right arm went back, snapped forward.

The disc sailed up in what seemed lazy flight—*too high*, thought Grimes, watching, *too high*.

Shirl stood there, making no attempt to throw a second one.

Grimes' boulder, under the impact of an armor-piercing bullet, split neatly down the middle, affording him a good view of what was happening. He saw the disc whir over Hephastia's position and then turn, dipping sharply downward as it did so. It vanished from sight.

There was one last shot, wildly aimed, which threw up a spray of mud between Grimes and the ship. There was a gurgling scream.

Calmly Shirl walked to where Grimes was sprawled in the mud, helped him to his feet.

"She will not bother you again, John," she said cheerfully.

"But how did you . . . ?"

He did not have to finish the question. The New Alicians had their telepathic moments.

"We did more than just sharpen the discs," she told him. "We used the grinding wheels and we . . . shaped them. Put in curves. Like boomerangs."

"But how did you *know* what to do?"

"We . . . We just *knew*."

Together they walked up the hillside, through the pouring rain, the others straggling after them. They came to the boulder from behind which Hephastia had been shooting. The sight of the fat woman's body was not quite as bad as Grimes had feared it would be; the downpour had already washed away most of the blood. Even so decapitation, or near decapitation, is never a pretty spectacle. Grimes looked away hastily from the gaping wound in the neck with the obscenely exposed raw flesh and cartilage. The rest of the body was not so bad. It looked drained, deflated, like a flabby white blimp brought to earth by heavy leakage from its gas cells. Her dead hands still held the rifle. Grimes took it from her. It was a 10 mm automatic, as issued to Federation military forces. It was set to Single Shot. There should have been plenty of rounds left in the magazine but there were not. Hephastia—or somebody—had neglected to replace it after some previous usage.

Grimes counted the remaining cartridges.

There were only five.

By this time the others had joined them.

"I've a rifle," said Grimes unnecessarily, "but only five rounds."

"There are weapons and ammunition a-plenty in the house," said Brasidus.

"Just what I had in mind," said Grimes.

He led the way up the hillside.

He covered the retreat, loosing off all five of the remaining rounds to deter a sally from the open door. The other women must have recovered, were firing from chinks in the heavily shuttered windows. After Grimes' warning burst they seemed to be reluctant to show themselves—much to the disgust of Shirl and Darleen.

"So," said Maggie, "what now?"

"We follow the river," said Grimes. "From what I can

remember of the maps there are sizable towns on its lower reaches."

"On *foot*?" squealed Fenella.

"You can try swimming if you like," said Grimes, "but I'd not recommend it with the river the way it is now."

Chapter 29

They were cold and they were wet and they were hungry.

Vividly in Grimes' memory was the smell of the cellar from which they had rescued Brasidus—the cheeses, the smoked and spiced sausages, the pickles. If only he had known that they were to be denied access to *Krait* he would have seen to it that they commenced what promised to be a very long walk well-provisioned and -armed.

Surprisingly Brasidus was not much help. Grimes had hoped that the Archon would have some idea of the geography of this area, would be able to guide them to some other village where there would be an inn, would be capable of finding for them the easiest and shortest route to the nearest town.

"But you're the ruler of this world!" said Grimes exasperatedly.

"That does not mean, friend John, that I know, intimately, every square centimeter of its surface, any more than you are familiar with every smallest detail of a ship that you command."

"I always do my best to gain such familiarity," grumbled Grimes.

They trudged on, the roaring torrent on their right, towering rocky outcrops, among which a few stunted trees struggled for survival, on their left. Grimes maintained the lead, with Maggie and Brasidus a little behind him, then Fenella, then Shirl and Darleen, the only ones with any sort of effective medium-range weaponry, as the rear guard. It was not likely that they would be followed but it was possible.

They trudged on.

They were no longer so cold; in fact they were sweating inside their heavy coveralls. The rain was easing. Now and again, briefly, the high sun struck through a break in the clouds.

But they were still hungry.

Grimes called a halt in the shelter of an overhanging cliff. He managed to light his pipe. (And how much tobacco was left in his pouch? He should have refilled it from a large container of the weed that Shirl had found for him in one of the officer's cabins aboard *Krait*.) Fenella had an almost full packet of cigarillos and, grudgingly, allowed Maggie to take one. Neither Brasidus nor the New Alician girls smoked.

Shirl and Darleen strayed away from the shelter, saying that they were going back up the trail a little to see if there were any signs of pursuit. Grimes let them go. He knew that they were quite capable of looking after themselves.

"And now," he said, "I'll put you in the picture, Brasidus. Prepare yourself for a shock."

"Ellena? Has anything happened to her?"

"On the contrary." Grimes laughed bitterly. "On the contrary. She's the one who's been making things happen. To begin with, she used your abduction as an excuse for seizing power."

Brasidus was not as shocked as Grimes had feared that he would be.

"She is a very shrewd politician, John, as I have known for quite awhile. And there has to be a strong hand at the helm during my forced absence. There are so many squabbling factions. . . ."

"But does she want you back?" asked Grimes brutally. "Oh, she didn't want you hurt but she did want you out of the way, does want you out of the way until she's firmly in the saddle. If she does allow you to come back it will be only as a sort of Prince Consort to her Queen Hippolyte."

Brasidus shook his head dazedly.

Then, at last, "You are trying to tell me that *she* is responsible for my abduction?"

"Yes," stated Grimes.

There was a long silence, broken eventually by the Archon.

"Yes," he muttered. "It does make sense, a quite horrible sort of sense. She *is* ambitious. She does really believe that she is a reincarnation of Queen Hippolyte. Her Amazon Guards are a formidable military force. Oh, I have sneered at them, as what man on this world has not, but, in my heart of hearts I have respected them. Those women back in the village were not Amazon Guards, had they been we should never have gotten out alive. They were no more than criminals whom somebody. . . ."

"Ellena," said Fenella.

"All right. Merely criminals hired by Ellena to do a job."

"Or loyal Party members," said Maggie, "following orders. Ellena's orders."

"Ellena, Ellena, always Ellena!" Brasidus got to his feet, began to pace up and down. "Always it comes back to Ellena."

"I'm afraid that it does," said Grimes.

"I should have known. As a ruler, as Archon, I have failed my people."

"Not yet," Grimes told him. "There are still people loyal to you."

They were interrupted by Shirl and Darleen. The two New Alicians were dragging something over the wet ground, something that might have been a very large snake had it not been equipped with eight pairs of legs. It was minus its head and the blood that dripped from its neck was an unpleasant yellow in color.

"Lunch," announced Shirl.

"Surely that *thing* is not edible," complained Fenella.

"It is," Brasidus told her, cheering up. "It is a delicacy. *Draco*, we call it. Broiled, with a fruit sauce. . . ."

Using their sharpened discs Shirl and Darleen lopped off the short legs of the draco, gutted and skinned it, throwing the offal into the river. Grimes tried to start a fire, using as fuel twigs broken from nearby bushes. But it was a hopeless task. All vegetation, even that in the partial shelter of the rock overhang, was thoroughly saturated and stubbornly refused to burn. If they had had an operating laser pistol at their disposal. . . . But they did not.

With a convenient flat rock as a table the New Alicians went on with their butchering. They sliced the flesh into wafer-thin slices. They gestured to Grimes that he should take the first bite.

He did. It wasn't bad, not unlike the sashimi that was a favorite meal of his when he could get it. It would have been vastly improved by a selection of dipping sauces but, he decided as he chewed, there were times when one couldn't have everything. Maggie joined him at the "table," then Fenella. Shirl and Darleen were already eating heartily. Only Brasidus hung back. (He, of course, was untraveled, had not sampled local delicacies on worlds all over the galaxy.)

"Try some," urged Grimes. "It's not bad."

"But it's not *cooked*."

"You must eat *something*," insisted Maggie, womanlike.

He forced himself to make a meal that obviously he did not enjoy.

Grimes ordered that the remains of the draco be thrown into the river. Now that the rain had ceased the day had become unpleasantly warm and already the meat was becoming odorous.

They pushed on down the mountainside.

It was early evening when they came to a village, larger than the one from which they had taken Brasidus. There was one short street, with low houses on either side of it. There was what looked like a small temple—to which deity of the Greek pantheon? wondered Grimes; it seemed to be of fairly recent construction—and, across the road from it, what was obviously an inn.

They entered this building, Brasidus in the lead.

There were several customers, all of them roughly dressed men, seated on benches at the rough wooden tables. These looked curiously at the intruders. There was the innkeeper, a grossly fat individual whose dirty apron strained over his prominent belly.

"Greetings, lords," he said. "What is your pleasure?"

"Wine," said Brasidus. "Bread. Hot meat if you have it."

"That indeed I have, lord. There is a fine stew a-simmering in the kitchen that would be fit for the Archon himself."

"Then bring it."

He bustled out, returned with a flagon of wine and six mugs, went out again for the platter of bread and individual bowls and spoons, and a last time for a huge, steaming pot from which issued a very savory smell.

"Eat well, my lords," he said. Then, "Have you been out in the storm?"

"We have," said Brasidus around a mouthful of stew.

"The weather was never like this when I was a boy. It's all these offworlders coming down in their ships, disturbing the clouds. Time was when there were only two ships a year, the ones from Latterhaven. . . ."

"Mphm," grunted Grimes, thinking that he had better make some contribution to the conversation.

"And what is the uniform that you are wearing, lords? Forgive my curiosity but we have so few visitors here. You have guns, I see. Would you be some sort of police officers?"

"We are in the Archon's service," said Brasidus, not untruthfully.

"Indeed? Would it be impertinent of me to inquire which branch?"

"It would."

This failed to register and the innkeeper rattled on.

"There are so many new branches these days. I've even heard tell that in Sparta City there's a *women's* army, and according to the last News we watched they're taking over. Troublous times, lords, troublous times. I'd not be surprised to learn that it's the women behind the vanishment of the Archon. We're old-fashioned folk here in Calmira. There are women here now, of course, but they know their places. They'd never come into the tavern. The temple's for them."

Fenella made an odd snorting noise.

"But it's getting quite dark, isn't it? It's all this weather we're having these days. I'll give you light to eat by; the power was off most of the day but it's back on now . . ."

He went to the switch by the door, clicked it on. The overhead light tubes were harshly brilliant. He returned to the table, stared at his guests, at Maggie, at Fenella, at Shirl and Darleen.

"You . . ." he sputtered. "*Women!*" he spat.

"So what?" asked Fenella coldly.

"But. . . . But never before in *my* inn. . . ."

"There has to be a first time for everything," she said.

He turned appealingly to Brasidus. "Had I known I'd never have admitted you."

"You know now," said Grimes. "And now you know, what can you do about it?"

The men at the other tables were stirring restively. There were mutterings of, "Throw them out! Throw them out!"

"Not before I've finished my meal," said Grimes.

"Throw them out!" It was more than just a muttering now.

Grimes put his spoon down in the almost empty bowl, took careful stock of the opposition. There were fourteen men, big men, not young but not old. They looked tough customers and, in the right (or wrong) circumstances, nasty ones. Of course, despite the numerical odds, there was little doubt as to what the outcome of a scuffle would be. Although there was no ammunition for the rifle, although the laser pistols were useless until recharged, there were still the stunguns, ideal for use in a situation such as this. And there were the two specialists in unarmed combat, Shirl and Darleen.

But. . . .

But one at least of the men might escape from the inn, might run to the Town Constable who, surely, would have some means of communication—radio or land line—with the nearest big town. And then Ellena would soon learn that her husband, with his low friends, was running around loose and that the failure of his guards to maintain communication with the Palace was due to more than storm damage.

"All right," he said to the innkeeper, "we'll go. But rest assured that a full report of this business will be made to the proper authorities."

"Then go," said the man. "But first. . . ."

He thrust a dirty piece of paper, the bill, under Grimes' nose. Grimes glanced at it. He did a mental conversion of obols into credits. He would have been charged less for a meal for six persons in many a four-star restaurant on many a world. Then he realized that, in any case, he could not pay. His wallet, with money and credit cards, was with the clothing that he had left aboard *Krait* when he changed into coveralls.

"Do you have any money on you?" he asked Maggie.

She shook her head.

"Fenella?"

"Back aboard the ship. Nothing here."

"Shirl? Darleen?"

"No."

"Are you paying, or aren't you?" demanded the innkeeper.

"You will have to send the bill to the Palace," Brasidus told him. "It will be honored."

"Check it first," said Grimes nastily.

"Send the bill to the Palace?" demanded the innkeeper. "What do you take me for? Who'll be in charge at the Palace by the time it gets there, the postal services being what they are these days? Tell me that."

A good question, thought Grimes.

He said, "If you insist, we'll leave security."

"What security?"

Another good question.

His wrist companion? wondered Grimes. *No.* It was too useful, with many more functions than those of a mere timekeeper. The same could be said for the instrument that Maggie was wearing on her left wrist. The ammunitionless rifle or the dead laser pistols? *Again no.* What police officer would cheerfully pass his weapons over to civilians in payment of a tavern bill? And, in any case, the laser pistols were clearly marked as Federation property.

He looked at the others around the table. A gleam of precious metal caught his eye.

He said, "I'll have to ask you for your watch, Fenella."

"*What?*"

"You'll be able to reclaim it after the bill's been paid."

"*If* it's ever paid."

"In which case you will be fully compensated."

Fenella extended her left hand. The innkeeper looked covetously at the fabrication of gold and precious stones thus displayed.

"Buying time with time," she said.

"I shall insist on a receipt," said Grimes.

One was reluctantly given, on a scrap of paper as dirty and as rumpled as the bill.

Then Grimes, Brasidus and the women went out into the gathering dark.

Chapter 30

Some distance downstream from the village they found a deserted hut.

It must once have been, suggested Brasidus, the abode of a goatherd. (The indigenous six-legged animals that had been called goats by the original colonists had been largely replaced, as food animals, by the sheep and cattle imported from Earth.) There was just one room, its floor littered with animal droppings and the bones of various small creatures that had been brought into this shelter by various predators to be devoured at leisure, that now crackled unpleasantly underfoot. By the flare of Maggie's and Fenella's lighters, set at maximum intensity, it was possible to take stock. There was, leaning against the wall, a crude beson. Shirl took this and began to sweep the debris out through the open door. There was a fireplace, and beside it what had once been a tidy pile of cut wood, now scattered by some animal or animals.

Grimes instructed Darleen to use the cutting edge of one of her discs to produce a quantity of thin shavings from one of the sticks. He laid a fire. The shavings took fire immediately from his match and the blaze spread to the thicker sticks on top. Too late he thought that he should have checked the chimney to see if it was clear but he need not have worried. The fire drew well. Although the night was still far from cold the ruddy, flickering light made the atmosphere much more cheerful.

They all sat down on the now more or less clean floor.

Grimes lit his pipe, estimating ruefully that he had barely enough tobacco left in his pouch for four more smokes. Maggie and Fenella made a sort of ritual of sharing a cigarillo. Shirl and Darleen sniffed disdainfully.

Maggie said, "Now what do we do? We're on the wrong side of this world with no way of getting back to Sparta City. We're wearing clothing that, as soon as the weather warms up, will be horribly uncomfortable and that, in any case, makes us conspicuous. We have no money . . ."

"And I no longer have my watch," Fenella said sourly. "What do we barter next for a crust of bread?"

"We shall have breakfast without any worry," said Shirl. She produced from the pouch in which she was carrying her throwing discs some rather squashed bread rolls and Darleen, from hers, some crumbling cheese. "Before we left the tavern we helped ourselves to what we could . . ."

"That will do for supper," said Grimes.

"There will be no supper," Maggie told him sternly.

She drew deeply on what little remained of the cigarillo, threw the tiny butt into the fire.

"Hold it!" cried Grimes—too late. "I could have used that in my pipe."

"Sorry," she said insincerely.

"We tried smoking once," said Darleen virtuously. "We did not like it. We gave it up."

Grimes grunted wordlessly.

"I'm not a porcophile," announced Fenella.

"What's that?" demanded Shirl.

"A pig-lover, dearie. Normally I've no time for the police, on any world at all. But I really think, that in our circumstances, we should turn ourselves in. After all, we've committed no crime. Oh, there was a killing, I admit—but it was self-defense . . ."

"And the 'borrowing' of a minor war vessel owned by the Interstellar Federation," said Grimes glumly. "A minor war vessel which, unfortunately, we are unable to return to its owners in good order and condition."

"But I was given to understand," persisted Fenella, "that you and Maggie have *carte blanche* in such matters."

"Up to a point," said Grimes. "A medal if things go well, a

court martial if they don't. In any case, until things get sorted out—if they ever do—Ellena will be able to hold us in jail on a charge of piracy and even to have us put on trial for the crime. And shot." He was deriving a certain perverse satisfaction from consideration of the legalities. "It could be claimed, of course, that I have been the ringleader insofar as the act of piracy is concerned. Don't forget that I have a past record. But you, Maggie, as a commissioned officer of the Survey Service, could be argued to have become a deserter from the FSS and an accessory before the fact to my crime. Shirl and Darleen are also accessories—and, also deserters from Ellena's own Amazon Guard. . . ."

"And me?" asked Fenella interestedly.

"An accessory before the fact."

"But it would never come to that," said Brasidus. "*I* shall vouch for you."

"Of course you will," said Grimes. "*But* . . . But if your lady wife is really vicious she'll put you on charge as an accessory after the fact."

"Surely she would not," said Brasidus. "After all, she is my wife."

"Throughout history," Fenella reminded him, "quite a few wives have wanted their husbands out of the way."

"But . . ."

"Are you sure that she wouldn't, old friend?" asked Grimes. He sucked audibly on his now empty pipe. "Now, this is the way I see things. We have to get less conspicuous clothing. By stealing. We have to get money. By stealing. Luckily this is a world where plastic money is not yet in common use. In the next town we come to there will be shops—I hope. Clothing shops. And there will be tills in these shops. With money in them. Luckily this is a planet where the vast majority of the population is honest, so breaking in will be easy. . . ."

"A bit of a come-down from space piracy," sneered Fenella.

"I wasn't a pirate," he said automatically. "I was a privateer."

Then he noticed that Shirl and Darleen had risen quietly to their feet and, as they had done so, had pulled their stunguns from their holsters. Shirl squatted by his side, put her mouth to his ear and whispered, "Go on talking. We shall be back in a few minutes."

Then she . . . oozed out of the open door, flattening herself against the frame to minimize her silhouette against the glow of the firelight. Darleen followed suit. Grimes went on talking, loudly so as to drown any queries from the others regarding the mysterious actions of the two New Alicians. He discussed at some length the legalities of privateering while his listeners looked at him with some amazement.

"It is not generally known," he almost shouted, "that the notorious Captain Kidd, who was a privateer, was hanged not for piracy but for murder, the murder of one of his officers. . . ."

"And what the hell has that to do with the price of fish?" screamed Fenella.

Shirl and Darleen came back. They were carrying between them an unconscious body, that of a man in the black leather and steel uniform of the Spartan Police. His arms were secured behind his back by his own belt and his ankles by the lacings of his sandals.

"We heard him coming," said Shirl, "while he was still quite a way off."

Brasidus stared at the man's gray-bearded face.

"I know him," he murmured. "I remember him from the old days, when we were both of us junior corporals. . . ."

"You've done better for yourself than he has," said Fenella.

"Have I? I'm beginning to think that I'd have been better off as a Village Sergeant than what I am now."

The journalist laughed. "You know, Brasidus, you're by no means the first planetary ruler who's said that sort of thing to me."

The Archon laughed too, but ruefully.

"But I," he said, "must be the first one who's really meant it."

Chapter 31

They sat and waited for the sergeant—whose name, Brasidus said, was Cadmus—to recover. Although the stunguns carried by Shirl and Darleen had been set to MINIMUM STUN the policeman had received a double dosage when ambushed by the New Alicians, being shot by both of them.

At last the man's eyes opened.

He stared bewilderedly at his captors. He struggled briefly
with his bonds but soon realized the futility of it. He looked from
face to face, longest of all at Brasidus.

He muttered, "I know *you*. . . ."

"And I know you, Cadmus," said the Archon.

"But. . . . But it can't be . . ."

"But it is."

"Brasidus. . . . Or should I be addressing you as Lord?"

"Brasidus will do. After all, we are old messmates."

"Brasidus. . . . But the news has been that you were kidnapped and that your lady wife has achieved power in your
absence from Sparta City . . . And now you are here, in my
village, in a strange uniform and in the company of . . . of
offworlders. *Women*."

"They are my friends, Cadmus. They rescued me. But tell
me—what are *you* doing here? Is there a police search for us?"

The sergeant laughed. "Not so far as I know. I was checking
up on an odd bunch of vagrants who had passed through my
village. You were not reported to me officially—the villagers are
a close-mouthed lot and regard the Police as an unnecessary
nuisance—but I overheard a few things and saw the innkeeper
wearing a *very* expensive watch. I questioned him and he finally
told me how he had got it. . . ."

"Did you get it back?" asked Fenella eagerly.

"No. The transaction, as he described it, seemed to be legal
enough. But do you think you could untie my wrists? I am very
uncomfortable."

There would be no harm in this, thought Grimes. The man had
been disarmed by Shirl and Darleen; his stungun was now stuck
into Darleen's belt and his scabbarded shortsword was being
worn by Shirl. Nonetheless he drew his own pistol and covered
the man while Darleen untied his lashings.

"That's better," said the sergeant, rubbing his wrists. Then,
to Brasidus, "Thank you, Lord."

"I've told you to call me Brasidus. After all, we're old
friends. How much does this friendship mean to you, Cadmus?
Could you help us? I promise you that if you do long overdue
promotion will follow."

"Don't insult me, Brasidus. I owe you for the way in which
you got me out of that mess some years ago . . . Remember?
When that little swine—what was his name? Hyperion?—got
himself killed resisting arrest, and he turned out to be Captain
Nestor's boyfriend. . . . No, Brasidus. I don't want promotion.

like being a Village Sergeant. All that I'd ask of you would be that I'd be appointed to a village of my own choice."

"But can you help us, Cadmus? We have to get back to Sparta City as soon as possible. We shall have to travel incognito. We shall need civilian clothing. Money. Transport . . ."

The sergeant laughed. "Let me tell you why I was looking for you. There's an order out that all offworlders, wherever they are, are to be rounded up and put in protective custody. They are to be returned to Sparta City and then put aboard the first outbound ship from Port Sparta. In this area Cythera, downriver from here, is the collection point. Trans-Spartan Airlines have a passenger ship standing by there to carry the offworlders to the spaceport."

"We shall still need clothing," said Grimes. "Something less conspicuous than what we are wearing now. And," he added hopefully, "a few obols spending money. Drinks. . . . Smokes. . . ."

"I have civilian clothing that I rarely use," said Cadmus. "I can fit out you, sir, and Brasidus." He looked the women over and chuckled to himself. "You'll not believe this," he went on, more to Brasidus than the others, "but I had a woman for a while. I wasn't all that sorry when she left me. She married a police lieutenant in Thebes. She left a few rags and I've never thrown them out. I thought they might come in handy some time."

Fenella laughed.

"And when *I* said, Grimes, that we should turn ourselves in to the police you smacked me down, and you had all these marvelous schemes involving breaking and entering and robbing shops . . . But the way it's turned out it's the police who're the only ones who can help us."

"But we didn't go to them," said Grimes. "They came to us."

"What was that about breaking and entering?" demanded Cadmus suspiciously.

"It was only a joke," Brasidus told him. "The lady has a peculiar sense of humor. Meanwhile, you *are* helping us, Cadmus. And you can help us best of all if you tell nobody, nobody at all, that you have found me. In your report to your superiors you will say only that you took charge of a group of six offworlders, two men and four women, and delivered them to the authorities in Cythera."

"It shall be done as you ask," said the sergeant as he undid the lashings about his ankles. He got unsteadily to his feet, assisted by Brasidus. "And now I must get back to my house to find the things that you require. I shall return at dawn, with the hovercar, to take you all to Cythera.''

"Perhaps we had better come with you," said Grimes.

"No," said Brasidus, "*no.*"

"But . . .''

"Never let it be said," declared the Archon, "that I do not trust my old friends.''

The trust was justified.

Before dawn Grimes was awakened by Shirl who, with Darleen, had shared sentry duty during what remained of the night. The New Alician's keen hearing had picked up the whine of ground effect engines while Cadmus was still a long distance off, long before Grimes could hear anything.

He got up from the hard floor, his joints stiff, his muscles aching. He ran a hand over his bristly chin, managed to ungum his eyelids. Shirl and Darleen had kept the fire going so there was light enough for him to see the others—Darleen curled in a fetal position, Maggie on her side, Fenella supine with her mouth open, softly snoring, Brasidus also on his back but as though sleeping at attention.

He would have sold his soul for a mug of steaming coffee or tea but there wasn't even any water. He filled and lit his pipe. He hoped that he would be able to purchase more tobacco in Cythera. He hoped that he would have some money on him to make such a purchase.

He awoke Brasidus, then the others. Only Brasidus—but he was already bearded—and Darleen looked none the worse for wear. Fenella was a mess. Maggie looked at least badly in need of a good hot shower and then a long session with her hairbrushes.

Grimes went outside and watered a tree. Then he stood and watched the approaching headlights of the police hovercar as it made its way down the winding trail. He had his stungun out, just in case. After a while he was joined by the others.

"He is a good man, that Cadmus," said Brasidus.

"Mphm," grunted Grimes.

"I would trust him with my life. More than once in the old days—in the old happy days—I did trust him with my life.''

"Hearts and flowers and soft violins," muttered Grimes.

"What do you mean, John?"

"Just a Terran saying.''

The hovercar came into view. It was a big vehicle. It sighed as it subsided in its skirts. One man, Cadmus, got out. He raised his right hand in greeting. Brasidus returned the salutation.

Cadmus said, "I have the things you need. If you will change now we can be on the way."

Shirl and Darleen lifted bundles from the rear of the car, carried them back into the hut. There was clothing as promised— rough tunics and heavy sandals for the men, chitons and lighter footwear for the ladies. There was a leather pouch full of clinking coins that Cadmus handed to Brasidus. And—which really endeared the sergeant to the commodore—there was a flagon of thin, sour wine, two dozen crisp rolls, still warm from the village bakery, and thick slices of some unidentifiable pickled meat. It was a far better meal than the bread and cheese which Shirl and Darleen had brought from the tavern would have been. *We should have had that for supper last night, as I wished,* thought Grimes.

Munching appreciatively he sat with the sergeant and watched the women changing. (On some worlds such conduct would have been unthinkable but New Sparta had no nudity tabu, any more than did the home planets of Maggie, Fenella, Shirl and Darleen.)

Cadmus jerked a thumb toward the New Alicians.

"Odd-looking wenches, aren't they? But not unattractive. Me— I've always liked a well-fleshed backside. . . ."

Backs to the bulkhead, thought Grimes, *when you're around.*

"Where're they from, sir? What is your name, by the way?"

"A world called New Alice," replied Grimes. "And my name is Smith. John Smith."

He got up, shed his own coveralls and boots, got into the tunic and sandals. He started to buckle on the belt with his weapons then thought better of it. Such accessories would look odd, to say the least, if carried by a bunch of stranded tourists.

He said, "You'd better take charge of these, Cadmus. And our coveralls."

The sergeant pulled a laser pistol from its holster, examined it, replaced it, then inspected one of the stunguns. He frowned.

"Both pistols," he said, "with Federation Survey Service markings. The laser with a flat power cell." He picked up a discarded coverall suit. "And a Survey Service heavy duty uniform . . ."

"I promise you," said Brasidus, "that I, personally, will tell you the full story later. But now I can and do tell you that there are things that it is better that you know nothing about."

"I can well believe that, Brasidus. And I think, at the risk of being deemed inhospitable, that the sooner I get you all off my hands, out of my territory, the better."

"We shall enjoy a happier reunion," Brasidus told him, "when things are back to normal."

"What *is* normal?" demanded the sergeant. "Nothing has been normal since that man Grimes came here in his ship all those years ago."

They bundled up the discarded clothing and carried it out to the car, stowing it in the baggage compartment, together with their belts and holstered pistols. The sun was up when they started off, with Brasidus sitting beside Cadmus, who was driving, and Grimes and the others in the rear cabin which was entirely enclosed, being intended for the occasional transport of arrested persons.

"Still," said Fenella, sitting back on the bench and extending her long, elegant legs, "it's better than walking. And now, Grimes, what's the drill when we get to Cythera? And what's the drill when we get back to Sparta City?"

"To begin with," Grimes told her, "my name is not Grimes. It's Smith. John Smith. And you're not Fenella Pruin . . ."

"Oh, all right, all right. I've been Prunella Fenn before."

"And I'm Angela Smith," announced Maggie.

"*Must* we have second names?" asked Shirl plaintively.

"Yes," Grimes told her. "Brown, for both of you. You're sisters."

"But we aren't."

"But you look alike. Shirley Brown and Dorothy Brown."

"Such *ugly* names!"

"But yours for the time being."

"I wish we could see some scenery," complained Maggie.

"If you *will* ride in the Black Maria, dearie," Fenella told her, "you can hardly expect a scenic drive. But go on, Grimes. Sorry. Smith. Tell us what world-shaking plots have merged from your tiny mind."

"I've seen this sort of thing before," said Grimes. "The handling and processing of refugees. The *real* processing won't be until we get to Sparta City. We'll tell the authorities at Cythera that we're a party of tourists who were set upon and robbed. The bandits took everything—money and, more importantly, our papers . . ."

"And your obviously expensive wrist companion," said Fenella, pointing at the device strapped to Grimes' left wrist.

"It will be out of sight in my pocket when we front the authorities," Grimes told her. "As will be Maggie's."

"I wish that my wristwatch had been in that bloody clip joint of an inn," she complained.

"You enjoyed the meal it paid for," Grimes told her.

"I noticed that *you* did," she snarled.

Chapter 32

They arrived at Cythera just before noon.

They saw little of the town itself—not that they much wished to—as Cadmus delivered them to the airport on its outskirts. There was a low huddle of administrative buildings. There were mooring masts, at one of which rode a Trans-Spartan dirigible. She was a small ship and a shabby one, her ribs showing through her skin. Grimes, looking up at her, was not impressed and said as much.

Just inside the airport's departure lounge was a desk at which was sitting a bored-looking police lieutenant. Cadmus saluted the officer and announced, "Six Terran tourists from Calmira, sir."

"And just in time, Sergeant. The ship will be embarking passengers in about ten minutes." He looked up at Grimes and his party. "Names? Identification papers?"

"They have no papers, sir," Cadmus told him. "They were robbed."

"You can say that again," muttered Fenella, the loss of whose wristwatch was still rankling.

"I trust that you will apprehend the miscreants responsible, Sergeant," said the officer, indicating by his manner that he could hardly care less.

"Investigations are being made, sir."

"And now, your names."

Grimes rattled these off, the Smiths and the Browns and the others. The lieutenant wrote them down on a form, said, "Thank you, Mr. Smith. And now just wait in the lounge with the other passengers. And that will do, Sergeant. You'd better be getting back to Calmira."

"Sir."

Grimes shook hands with Cadmus.

"Thank you for your help, Sergeant. I shall see to it that the Terran Ambassador knows about what you have done for us."

"It was only my duty, sir."

Brasidus shook hands with Cadmus.

Shirl and Darleen, while the lieutenant looked on disgustedly, flung their arms about him and planted noisy kisses on his cheeks. (They had aimed for his mouth but he managed to turn his head just in time.)

Grimes led the way into the lounge. He had spotted a refreshment stall. ("But they'll feed us aboard the ship . . ." protested Maggie.) As he had hoped, there were smokes of various kinds on sale. He bought a tin of tobacco of an unknown brand, paying for it out of the money provided by Cadmus. Now he could afford to fill his pipe properly from what remained in his pouch. He lit up and surveyed those who were to be his fellow passengers on the flight to Sparta City. There were, he estimated, about sixty of them. There was a group of Waverley citizens, male and female, who had stubbornly refused to go native insofar as apparel was concerned and were clad in colorful kilts in a wide variety of tartans. There were fat ladies from Earth for whom chitons did nothing but to make a desperate attempt to hide their overly abundant nakedness and their skinny husbands, looking, in their skimpy tunics, like underdressed scarecrows. There were the inevitable young people with their rucksacks and short shorts and heavy hiking boots. There were, even, three Shaara, a princess and two drones, surveying the motley throng through their huge, faceted eyes with arthropodal arrogance.

"And how long will it take that gasbag to get us to Sparta City?" asked Fenella.

"Three days is my guess," said Grimes.

"Ugh! In this company!"

The public address system came to life. "All offworlders will now leave the lounge by departure gate three. All offworlders will now leave the lounge by departure gate three. Small hand baggage only."

People began to straggle out from the lounge, along the paved path to the mooring mast, escorted by policemen who tried to hurry things up.

"I'll never come here again for a holiday!" Grimes overheard. "They take our money, then treat us like criminals!"

"But you must make allowances, dear. They're in the middle of the revolution."

"Then why the hell couldn't they have waited to have it when we were safely back home?"

By groups the tourists took the short elevator ride up to the top of the mooring mast, passed through the tubular gangway into the body of the ship. Flight attendants, surly men in shabby uniforms, chivvied them aft into a large cabin. There were rows of seats, of the reclining variety. There was, Grimes realized with a sinking heart, no sleeping accommodation. Obviously this was normally a short-haul passenger carrier pressed into service for the transport of those who were, now, little better than refugees.

Grimes, Brasidus and Maggie shared a bank of three seats on the port side of the cabin. Fenella and Shirl and Darleen sat immediately behind them. The cabin filled up.

No announcement was made when the flight commenced. There was no friendly "This is your captain speaking." There was just a faint vibration as the motors were started and, through the viewport in the ship's skin, the sight of the ground below receding.

Shortly thereafter a meal was served—bowls of greasy stew, stale rolls and muddy coffee. It made a sordid beginning to what was to be a sordid voyage.

Grimes, who was something of an authority on the history of transport, was to say later that it was like a long trip must have been in the Bad Old Days on Earth, during that period when the fuel-guzzling giant airplanes reigned supreme in the skies, before the airship made its long deferred comeback as a passenger carrier. There were the inadequate toilet facilities. There was the flavorless food, either too greasy or too dry, or even, both at once. There was the canned music. There were the annoying restrictions surely imposed by some fanatical non-smoker.

"It took absolute genius," he would say, "to reproduce aboard a modern dirigible, the only civilized means of aerial transport, conditions approximating those in Economy Class aboard an intercontinental Jumbo Jet of the late Twentieth Century. . . ."

What made it even worse for him was that he was not used to traveling as a passenger, or as a passenger not accorded control room privileges. As Commodore Grimes he would have spent most of the flight in the ship's nerve center, observing, asking intelligent questions, conversing with the captain and officers. As Mr. Smith he was just one of the herd, livestock to be carted from Point A to Point B and delivered in more or less good order and condition.

It was impossible for him to have proper conversations with his companions, to discuss the course of action once they had disembarked at the Sparta City airport. There were too many around them who could overhear, including the flight attendants. From one of these they managed to obtain some paper and a stylus—the man had to be tipped—on the pretext of playing word games. They passed notes between their two rows of seats, hidden between the sheets of airline stationery upon which there were a sort of crude variation of Scrabble.

They ate, forcing the food down. They slept as well as they could. They listened to the loud—and mostly fully justified—complaints of the other passengers. They made bets on the frequency with which a particularly annoying, tritely sweet melody would come up on the canned music program. And, with the others, they became steadily scruffier and scruffier. The acridity of stale perspiration became the most dominant odor in the cabin's atmosphere. It needed, said Grimes loudly, a strong injection of good, healthy tobacco smoke to purify it.

Their communication by written messages did not produce any worthwhile results. As Grimes said in his final note, after arrival at Sparta City they would just have to play by ear.

At last, at long, long last, the airship's captain broke his voyage-long silence.

"Attention, all passengers. We are now approaching our mooring at Sparta City Airport. After mooring has been completed you will disembark in an orderly manner and put yourselves into the care of the authorities. That is all."

Grimes stared out through the port. The airship was making a wide sweep over the city. Surely, he thought, it was not usually as dark as this. The winding streets were no more than feeble trickles of sparsely spaced lights. The Acropolis was no longer floodlit. But around the Palace there was glaring illumination. And what were those flashes? Gunfire?

He asked one of the surly flight attendants the local time. It was 0400 hours. When the man was out of sight he took his wrist companion from his pocket and set it. Even though he would not be keeping a written log of events he always liked to know just when whatever was happening was happening.

The city lights fell slowly astern.

The vibration of the motors became less intense, then ceased. Sundry clankings came from forward as the ship was shackled to her mast.

"We're here," said Grimes unnecessarily.

"Thank all the odd gods of the Galaxy for that," said Maggie.

Chapter 33

At the foot of the mooring mast there was a small detachment of bored looking police, obviously resentful at having to be up at this ungodly hour. They herded the disembarking passengers into a lounge where a sullen lieutenant ticked their names off on a list. The only persons at whom he looked at all closely were the three Shaara. They stared him down.

Coffee and little sweet buns were available. It was not the sort of refreshment which Grimes would have ordered had he any choice in the matter, but it was far better than the meals aboard the airship.

Sipping and munching, he stood close to three of the policemen.

"All this extra duty . . ." one was complaining. "And then, on top of it all, we have to be at the bloody Acropolis at ten in the bloody morning for the bloody coronation. If *she* is as bloody popular as she says she is, why does she want *us* to guard her? What's wrong with her own bloody Amazon Guard? Answer me that."

"Politics, Orestes, politics. Wouldn't do, this early, if she showed herself relying too heavily on her own pet tabbies. For all this Queen Hippolyte reincarnation crap she wants to be crowned ruler of all Sparta, not of just one sex. But once she's firmly in the saddle, then we shall see what we shall see."

"What d'ye suppose *did* happen to Brasidus?" asked the third man. "With all his faults, he wasn't a bad bastard."

"Done away with, of course," said the expert on politics. "We'll never see *him* again."

"And more's the pity," muttered the first man.

Grimes drifted away to where the others were seated in a corner of the lounge, close to one of the big sliding windows. There was nobody else within earshot.

"Maggie, your bug detector," he said in a low voice. "It could be safe to talk here, but I want to be sure . . ."

147

She took the instrument out of her pocket, pressed buttons, watched and listened.

She said, "All right. We can talk."

"To begin with," said Grimes, "Ellena's going to be crowned this morning. Queen of all Sparta. At ten."

"I can't believe that!" growled Brasidus.

"I'm afraid that you have to, old friend. The question is—do you want to stop her?"

"Yes. Yes. After all, she is only a woman."

Fenella's indignant squawk must have been audible all over the airport—but there had already been so many loud complaints from other passengers that it went almost unnoticed.

"*I* am the Archon," went on Brasidus. "Now I am back where I belong. I shall resume my high office without delay."

"Go for broke . . ." muttered Grimes.

"What was that, John?"

"Just a Terran expression. It means . . ." He fumbled for the right words. "It means that you stake everything on a single throw of the dice."

"I like that," said Brasidus. "I like that. And are you with me, John? And you, Maggie?"

"What about asking me?" demanded Fenella.

"And us?" asked Shirl and Darleen.

"Very well. Are you with me? All of you."

"Yes," they all said.

"First of all," said Grimes, "we have to get out of the airport. That shouldn't be difficult. After all, we aren't prisoners. Nobody regards a bunch of offplanet refugees as being potentially dangerous."

"And then we make for the Palace," said Brasidus.

"Do we?" asked Grimes. "With all due respect to your lady wife, Brasidus, I wouldn't trust her as far as I could throw her. And she is not a small woman. The way I see it is this. We go underground for a while until we find out which way the wind is blowing."

"But *you* said 'go for broke,' John. There has to be a confrontation between myself and Ellena. Oh, I should never have married her—I've known that for quite some time—and, however things turn out, I shall not stay married to her for much longer." All the built-up bitterness was coming out in a rush. "There must be a confrontation. A *public* confrontation so that the people can make their own choice between us. At the coronation."

"Mphm," grunted Grimes. *Go for broke,* he thought. *Why*

not? If things didn't work out he could get a message out—somehow—to *Sister Sue* and she could come in and lift him and the others off New Sparta. If, that is, they woud be, by that time, in any condition to be lifted off. But his luck had held so far. Why should it not hold for a little longer?

As inconspicuously as possible they drifted out of the lounge, first to the toilet facilities. In a cloakroom Shirl and Darleen found a pair of long cloaks that would conceal their not-quite-human bodies from curious eyes. Nobody stopped them when they found a door opening to the outside. The night, what was left of it, was almost windless. The clear sky was ablaze with stars.

Once they were clear of the airport Brasidus—after all, it was his city—led the way. The first part of their long walk was through orchards of some kind; the spicy scent of ripening fruit was heavy in the still air. Then they entered a built-up area. Shirl and Darleen, with their keen hearing, picked up the whine of an approaching hovercar before any of the others. They all found concealment in a side alley until the vehicle—a police patrol chariot?—was past. The next time they had to hide was from a detachment of soldiers on foot. Now and again they heard the rattle of automatic projectile weapons. Once they stumbled—literally—across a dead body, that of a policeman. His pistol holsters, Grimes discovered to his disappointment, were empty.

Then it was dawn and, only a little later, sunrise. People were emerging into the street, unshuttering shop windows. Presumably the coming of daylight signalled the lifting of the curfew.

Brasidus found an inn. Before leading the way into it he checked the remaining contents of the money pouch that Cadmus had given him, said there should be enough for breakfast for all of them. Grimes told him that he would have to do the ordering as he was the only one without a foreign accent. (But there were now so many Spartan citizens recently arrived from other planets that this did not much matter.)

They took seats at a table. They were the only customers. The sullen waitress made it obvious that she resented this disruption of her early morning peace and quiet. There were quite a few items on the blackboard menu that Grimes would have liked—even eggs and bacon!—but the girl told them that the cook was not yet on duty. She produced the inevitable muddy coffee—yesterday's brew, warmed up—and stale rolls.

Other people drifted in.

These were regulars and received better treatment than the strangers had gotten. Their coffee smelled as though it had been freshly made and their rolls looked fresh. The waitress put on a pleasant face and joined in conversations.

"No, I shan't be going to the coronation. Wouldn't go even if I could get time off. That Ellena and her bunch of dykes! But I liked Brasidus. He was a *real* man. . . ."

"They say," contributed a male customer, "that Ellena had him quietly murdered."

"It's time somebody murdered her," muttered his friend.

"Careful," whispered the third man. "You can never tell who's listening these days . . ."

All three of them scowled suspiciously at Grimes and his party.

Brasidus called for the bill. He had enough money to cover it. He paid.

On the way out Grimes heard one of the men ask the girl, "And who were *they*?"

"Dunno. Never seen 'em before. Don't care much if I ever see 'em again."

"Shouldn't mind seein' more o' those wenches," said the first man.

"Probably Amazon Guard officers in civvies," said the second.

"Shut up!" hissed the girl, noticing that Grimes was lingering in the doorway, listening. "Shut up, you fool!"

After their breakfast they had time to spare. They sauntered through the city, playing the part of country cousins enjoying a good gawk. They saw streetcorner meetings being broken up by police—and noticed that, uncharacteristically, the law officers were using force only when absolutely necessary and then with seeming reluctance. They heard orators, female as well as male, screaming their support for Brasidus and demanding that he return to bring things back under control.

On more than one wall there were slogans crudely daubed.

ELLENA GO HOME! was a common one.

Brasidus laughed bitterly. "That's what I've been thinking for years but I've never said it out loud. Now I am saying it. I promise you—and promise myself—that once I'm back in control Ellena will be shipped back to Earth by the first available vessel. Does that ship of yours have any passenger accommodation, John?"

"No," lied Grimes.

"It doesn't matter. A spare storeroom would be good enough for *her*."

Not aboard my *ship*, thought Grimes.

They dropped into a tavern for wine, using the last of Cadmus' money to pay for it. They mingled with the crowds—women, men, not too many children—who were converging upon the Acropolis. Shirl and Darleen took the lead; they had the ability to flow through and past obstructions like wild animals through dense undergrowth. Even so, it was not all that easy for Grimes and the others to keep up with them. Altercations broke out in their wake as toes were trodden and ribs painfully nudged.

But, eventually, they were standing in the front row, at the foot of the wide marble steps, facing a rank of black-uniformed police, all of whom had their stunguns drawn and ready. The dais at the head of the steps, with the white pillars of the Acropolis as its backdrop, was still empty. To either side of it were the news media cameras, at this moment slowly scanning the crowd.

Trumpets sounded and there was a rhythmic mutter of drums. The cameras turned to cover Ellena's grand entry. She strode majestically to the dais, flanked by high-ranking military officers, both male and female, followed by white-robed Council members. Among these was a tall woman on whose right shoulder rode an owl. Grimes stared at this. It was a real bird. It blinked, shifted its feet, half lifted its wings.

"The High Priestess of Athena," whispered Brasidus.

The trumpets were silent but the drums maintained a soft throbbing. Ellena stood there, waiting for the applause that was supposed to greet her appearance. She was a majestic enough figure in Amazon Guard uniform, more highly polished bronze than leather. Her plumed helmet added to her already not inconsiderable height. She stood there, frowning.

At last, from somewhere in the crowd, there was an outbreak of cheering and cries of, "Ellena! Ellena!" But there was also some booing. And were the people, wondered Grimes, who were chanting, "Hip, Hip, Hippolyte!" applauding or exercising their derision?

Trumpets blared.

Ellena raised her arms, brought her hands to her shining helmet, lifted it from her head, handed it to an Amazon aide. A white-robbed acolyte gave an elaborate crown of golden laurel leaves to the High Priestess, who advanced to stand beside Ellena. Beside her stood one of the councillors, an elderly man, stooped, feeble, with wrinkled face and sparse white hair.

He spoke into a microphone. Despite the amplification his voice was feeble.

"Citizens of Sparta. . . . We are gathered together on this

A. Bertram Chandler

great and happy occasion to witness the coronation of our first Queen. . . . In accordance with our Law the appointment of the ruler must be by public consent. . . . Do any of you gathered here know of any reason why the Lady Ellena should not be crowned Queen of all Sparta?''

"She's a woman, that's why!" yelled somebody.

But Ellena was now seated on the thronelike chair that had been brought for her and the High Priestess, standing behind it, had the golden crown raised in her hands, ready to lower it on to Ellena's head.

"For the second time," quavered the elderly councillor, "do any of you gathered here know of any *valid* reason why the Lady Ellena should not be crowned Queen of all Sparta?"

"We want Brasidus! We want Brasidus!" quite a number of voices were chanting.

"For the third and the last time, do any of you gathered here . . .''

"We want Brasidus! We want Brasidus! We want the Archon! We want the Archon!"

Brasidus cried in a great voice, "I am Brasidus! I am the Archon!"

Freakishly the microphones caught his words, sent them roaring over the crowd. The news media cameras swiveled to cover him. The policemen at the foot of the vast staircase shifted away to the sides as he began his advance to confront his wife.

Ellena was back on her feet, furious, pointing an accusatory hand.

"Guards! Kill this impostor!"

Her own Amazons might well have obeyed but the military personnel in her immediate vicinity were all men. Grimes recognized one of the officers although it was the first time that he had seen him in uniform. It was Paulus.

"Guards!" Ellena was screaming now. "Kill this impostor!"

"Brasidus!" the crowd was roaring. "Brasidus!"

On the platform Ellena was yelling at Paulus. "Shoot him, you useless bastard! Shoot him!"

"But he is the Archon."

"He is an impostor!" She wrestled briefly with the man who had been Brasidus' bodyguard, succeeded in pulling a heavy projectile pistol from the holster at his belt, smote him on the forehead with the barrel, knocking him to the ground. "All right!" she snarled. "If none of you will do the job, *I* will!"

She raised the weapon, holding it in both hands. It was obvious that she knew how to use it.

From the corner of his eye Grimes caught a blur of movement to his right, the glint of sunlight reflected from bright metal. Darleen had pulled one of the deadly sharpened discs from the pouch that she was still carrying. With a snap of her wrist she launched it. When it hit its target Ellena was about to squeeze off her first shot. The report of the pistol was shocking, deafening almost, but where the bullet went nobody ever knew.

Ellena screamed.

And then she was standing there, with blood spouting from her ruined right hand, still clinging to the pistol, still trying to bring it to bear, although it was obvious that those more than half severed fingers would never be able to pull a trigger until extensive and lengthy repair work had been carried out.

People joined Brasidus in his march up the steps to the platform, some in civilian clothing, some in police and army uniforms. There was scuffling among the assembled dignitaries but no shots were fired. The Amazon Guard officers were doing their best to stand haughtily aloof, striking out, damagingly, only when jostled. Their loyalty, thought Grimes with some bewilderment, was to their Corps, not to Ellena. She must have done something to antagonize them.

(Later, very much later, he was to learn that Ellena intended to lay the blame for her husband's murder on top-ranking Amazon officers, who were to be executed after a mere parody of a trial. Somehow they had discovered this and already had their own plans for Ellena's elimination. But now she was saving them the trouble.)

Ellena had collapsed and was receiving medical attention.

Brasidus had gained access to a microphone. "Fellow citizens! People of Sparta, men and women both! I have returned. Later the full story of my abduction and my rescue by very good friends will be told to you. . . ."

Grimes didn't catch the rest of it.

He had been accosted by a man whom at first he thought was a stranger, a slightly built fellow with a dark complexion, dressed in ill-fitting civilian clothes.

"You bastard! You bloody pirate!" this person sputtered. "What did you do with my ship?"

"It's a long story," said Grimes at last. "But I'll see to it that you get her back, Lieutenant Gupta."

Chapter 34

And Grimes got his own ship back when, at last, *Sister Sue*
dropped down to Port Sparta. He got his name back on to the
Register as Master and Billy Williams, surprisingly cheerfully,
reverted to his old rank as Chief Officer, saying, "Now you can
have all the worries again, Skipper."

And worries there were.

Discharge of cargo had just begun when a strongly worded
request—it was more of an order, really—came from Admiral
Damien by Carlotti deep space radio. This was that Grimes
handle the salvage of *Krait*. He had done this sort of job before,
back on Botany Bay, and the courier was a very small ship and
Sister Sue had plenty of power and, even with most of her cargo
still on board, could have lifted *Krait* bodily. As it was, throughout the operation the courier's stern remained in contact with the
ground. And then she had to be stayed off so that she was safely
stable while Grimes' engineers made repairs to her engines.

One consolation was that as Grimes, officially, was no longer
connected with the Survey Service he would be able to put in a
large bill for the services of himself and his ship.

And now his Earthbound cargo was almost loaded and, very
soon now, *Sister Sue* would be secured for space.

Maggie sat with Grimes in his day room.

"And so," she said, "our ways part again."

"It was good while it lasted," he said.

"Yes."

"You could resign your commission," he told her, "and enter
my employ."

"You resigned yours, John, but they pressganged you back
into servitude. And my orders are that I must remain on New
Sparta until the situation has stabilized. And. . . . And you must
have noticed how things are now between Brasidus and myself."

"How could I not have noticed?"

154

"But you must understand, my dear, that it's all part of the job. *My* job. He must be taught that all women aren't like Ellena. . . ."

"Is that all?"

"No. I admire Brasidus. I'm sorry for him. And, if you must know, I love him in my fashion. But as soon as I have him back on an even keel—and as soon as this planet's back on an even keel—I shall be on my way. I've no doubt that Damien will find another job for me."

"To judge from my own experience of the old bastard, no doubt at all. But what a can of worms this one turned out to be!"

"And now that the chief worm has been removed the others should quiet down. But what a cunning bitch she was! Playing both ends against the middle. *Both* ends? I still have to find out just how many ends there were. And if it hadn't been for her plans to purge the high command of her own Amazon Guard she might still have pulled it off."

"How *did* Colonel what's-her-name find out what was in store for her?"

"You and I, John, were by no means the only intelligence operatives on New Sparta, although we were the only Survey Service ones. I had my contacts."

"You might have told me."

"The less you knew," she said, "the better."

"Mphm."

"Cheer up. You've got your ship back. Thanks to me you won't be getting Ellena as a passenger. I persuaded Brasidus that a dangerous woman such as her should be sent back to Earth in a warship, where she can be kept under guard. The destroyer *Rigel* will have the pleasure of her company. As you know, she's due in a couple of days after you lift off."

"I thought for a while that I might have the dubious pleasure of Fenella's company."

"She decided that there are still stories to be had on New Sparta. Too, she's set her sights on Brasidus." She laughed. "I might even let her have him. Who better to retail the scandalous gossip of a palace than one who's the subject of such gossip herself?"

"Mphm," grunted Grimes again. *Brasidus*, he thought a little jealously, *was doing very nicely for himself, getting his hairy paws onto all of Grimes' women. . . .*

There was a knock at the door.

"Enter!" called Grimes.

The door opened. Billy Williams stood there.

"Secured for space save for the after airlock, Skipper," he reported. "The two passengers, with their gear, have just boarded."

"*Passengers*, Mr. Williams?"

"I thought you knew, sir. A lady officer from the Palace, an Amazon major, came out with them and told me that everything had been arranged."

Two familiar forms appeared in the doorway behind the Chief Officer.

"Hi!" said Shirl (or was it Darleen?).

"Hi!" said Darleen (or was it Shirl?).

Maggie got to her feet, then bent to kiss Grimes as he still sat in his chair.

"See you," she said. "Somewhere, somewhen."

Billy Williams left with her to escort her to the airlock.

"Aren't you pleased to see us?" asked the two New Alicians as one.

Grimes supposed that he was.

PHILIP K. DICK

"The greatest American novelist of the second half of the 20th Century."

—*Norman Spinrad*

"A genius . . . He writes it the way he sees it and it is the quality, the clarity of his Vision that makes him great."

—*Thomas M. Disch*

"The most consistently brilliant science fiction writer in the world."

—*John Brunner*

PHILIP K. DICK

In print again, in DAW Books' special memorial editions:

☐ **WE CAN BUILD YOU** (#UE1793—$2.50)
☐ **THE THREE STIGMATA OF PALMER ELDRITCH**
(#UE1810—$2.50)
☐ **A MAZE OF DEATH** (#UE1830—$2.50)
☐ **UBIK** (#UE1859—$2.50)
☐ **DEUS IRAE** (#UE1887—$2.95)
☐ **NOW WAIT FOR LAST YEAR** (#UE1654—$2.50)
☐ **FLOW MY TEARS, THE POLICEMAN SAID** (#UE1624—$2.50)